MW00981586

Titan 2:
City Under Siege

HUGH BECKSTEAD

Illustrations by
Jena Stillwell

Hugh Beckstead

RED APPLE

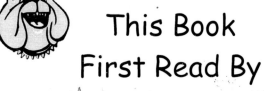

This Book
First Read By

Michael Bonface

2013 Hugh Beckstead

All rights reserved.

ISBN: 1494251299
ISBN-13: 978-1494251291

Acknowledgments

As with the first Titan book I had plenty of help in completing this one. I would really like to thank everyone who assisted me in reading and editing this manuscript in all its different forms. I could not have done it without your support.

Wanda Gibbons, I greatly appreciate all of your insight and comments. I appreciate all your support you gave me throughout this whole process so much. You have been encouraging me to write one way or another since junior high. Rick and Diane Kelly, you have both been so supportive and always ready to help and be there with anything I have done for this book, I cannot thank you enough. Greg Langham, thank you so much for all of your in depth insight. And Maureen Mieras, thank you for pointing out all of the `AS` going on. Jim Henry and Red Apple Publishing, thanks for everything, from the website down to the e-book format help. Thank you all, you helped make this a much better book than I could have done on my own.

To my parents, who always said they would support me in whatever I chose to do. And my sister, Shannon, who showed me how to have courage and be a superhero.

And to my wife, Carly, you have supported me from the very beginning, and continue to be my biggest fan. I owe so much of who I have become to you. I love you always and forever

CONTENTS

Previously

After witnessing a police chase that was the result of a museum heist, teenager Michael Novak discovers a magical ring that transforms him into the superhero Titan. With the help of spirit guide Azure, Titan is charged with battling the forces of evil wherever they should arise. The main source of evil in Michael's home of Delta City was the mysterious criminal kingpin Mr. Midnight.

Mr. Midnight had developed a new weapon, a handheld device known as the motion inhibitor that could immobilize people for up to ninety minutes. He had also developed a mass motion inhibitor that would allow him to immobilize large portions of the entire city at once, unless Titan could stop him.

Michael however was finding it hard balancing the life of a regular teenager and the secret identity of a superhero. The only person who knew he was Titan was his girlfriend, Carly. Michael couldn't even share this news with his best friends or blind grandfather. Though, being Titan lead Michael to discover some disturbing truths about his bully of an older brother, Vince. Vince seemed to be directly linked to the criminal activities of Mr. Midnight.

After battling the fiery villain Inferno, who was dispatched by Mr. Midnight, Michael learns a valuable lesson as Carly was on hand to witness the fight, and was also in jeopardy during the battle.

Titan did manage to make one ally in his battle against evil, and that was with plucky reporter Vicki Earnhardt. Titan and Vicki agreed to feed firsthand accounts of his exploits to her in exchange of information on criminal activities that she knows about in the city. It is from Vicki that Titan learns about Mr. Midnight.

Finally, Titan faced off against Mr. Midnight and his crew in an old warehouse just as they were about to launch the mass inhibitor. Titan destroyed the inhibitor and the warehouse, saving the city. In the chaos Mr. Midnight vanished and was believed dead, but no one knows for sure. For the time being, however, Delta City was safe and Vince was hopefully scared straight thanks to Titan.

CHAPTER 1: Shock and Awe

Even being three blocks away, Titan could feel the force of the explosion. The building he was sprinting across began to shake and tremble. Straight ahead he could see the night sky light up in a brilliant shade of orange and red as a giant billowing cloud of fire rose up into the air. Just as he reached the edge of the building's rooftop, Titan dropped his head down, took three more great strides, bent his knees and launched himself high into the air toward the explosion.

Titan, I believe we have found the sign we have been looking for. We must reach the destination of that explosion before we lose them again. Knowing their penchant for watching their handy work, Shock and Awe will still be there, but we have little time to spare.

Azure's voice had come right on cue. Over the last several months Titan and Azure had developed a strong rapport fighting crime. Titan had come to know just when Azure would speak and what he would generally say. That is not to say however that he never had problems understanding how or why he said certain things. Yet, he supposed, that is just how it goes when you're taking advice on being a teen superhero from an ancient disembodied voice in your head. Titan knew there were just certain things about having special superpowers that he would just never fully understand.

"I see it, Azure," Titan said, as he bent and angled his body high over the financial district of Delta City. Wind and warm air from the explosion began to envelope him as he drew closer to the blast.

Shock and Awe had been wreaking havoc across the city for the past week. They were twin brother and sister pyro maniacs that both stood only five feet tall, and Titan was determined to put a stop to them once and for all.

"I just hope this isn't some sort of trap like the last one. I don't want to get blasted out of the sky," said Titan.

Yes, let us hope not. You should draw your staff and be on guard for anything.

Titan tensed his body as he prepared to land in the middle of an intersection adjacent to the building that was once the First National Bank of Delta City. It was a mass of rubble engulfed in flames. Blocking one of the streets from the intersection was a giant panel van with an elaborate mechanical setup on its roof and sides. It looked like the whole van was a giant bomb on wheels. Standing on the roof of the van were two small figures. Clad in dark glasses and yellow fire retardant suites. They resembled a pair of nightmarish firefighters.

Titan stood surveying the van. The two figures on top either did not notice him or did not care to. They simply faced the burning building staring into the flames. With several other fires of similar size already this night, Titan knew it might take the Delta City Fire Department a little extra time to get to this new blaze.

"Shock and Awe!" Titan hollered getting the figures attention. "You two are done, now!"

"Oh, I don't think so. How about you, sis?" said the slightly bulkier of the two figures.

"But Shock, we can't be done before we blow our big surprise," said Awe.

"Sorry, masked avenger," Shock said, turning back to Titan. "I don't think we can let you take us that easy."

"You know, I just don't get you two. I mean, most criminals would look to rob a bank before they blow it to smithereens, but not you two. Is this some sort of weird twins' thing I don't know about or are you two just extra weird?" questioned Titan.

"Brother, did you hear the little boy in the Halloween costume insult us?" sneered Awe.

"I did, sister. Maybe he doesn't know that we don't want to rob his fair city, we want to watch it burn," asserted Shock.

Titan tensed, sensing things were about to get a little more interesting very quickly, and that he may have just walked into a trap. He clenched his staff tightly. His other hand was wrapped in a fist. Azure was being unusually silent.

Suddenly Awe dropped down into the back of the van. An opening appeared in the side of the van and several small round objects with flashing red lights shot out at Titan. The three objects fanned in an arc aimed straight at him. Titan pulled back his staff and batted the first two away. One flew into the air, exploding with a small bang like a grenade, doing no property damage. The other flew through the window of a parked car blowing the top completely off. Titan was not fast enough for the third. It blew into his side sending him flying through the brick wall on his left into a small luncheonette that, thankfully, was closed. Sharp pain stabbed at his side and then quickly subsided. His legs were buried under a small pile of brick as he lay propped up by his arms.

"Well, I think it's time to bring out some heavy artillery of my own," Titan said, as he pulled himself from the rubble.

Titan, I do not advise that you use the lightning from your staff. You don't know what kind of explosives they may have in that van and we don't want to destroy the entire area.

"Fine, but just so you know, this could get ugly."

As Titan climbed through the hole in the wall he could finally hear the approaching sound of fire engine sirens. He knew he had to act fast. The last thing he wanted was to have any firefighters caught in the cross fire with Shock and Awe.

"We will destroy you, Titan, and then we will blow up as much of Delta City as we can," Shock said, still standing on the van's roof and pointing one stubby little finger at Titan.

Suddenly the electrical panels attached to the side of the van began to come alive with blinking red lights and various bleep and bloop sounds. The side panel of the van facing Titan then extended away from the entire body of the van, detached and dropped to the ground. Now he could clearly see Awe sitting inside the van at a control console, hitting levers and buttons. As Titan realized what was going on, he noticed Shock turn and begin to climb back inside. Awe was making her way to the cab of the van. It took Titan a moment to register that the twins had just dropped a bomb in the middle of the street.

Titan, that is clearly a very powerful bomb. We must dispose of it quickly.

"I can't let them get away again."

We have no way of knowing how much damage that bomb could cause. There are emergency response workers on their way; the bomb must be our first priority.

"Okay, fine, but I don't want you to say anything if they get away and have another chance to do this again," Titan responded, cautiously moving toward the bomb.

Titan carefully lifted the dropped panel over his head. Out of the corner of his eye he saw the two twisted twins, now positioned in the cab, fire up the engine. Awe's eyes went wide as she saw Titan lift the heavy panel overhead. Titan squatted and then leaped straight into the air with the bomb. He kept his gaze down at first and saw the van make its getaway. Just above the city level, Titan pulled the panel back and threw the bomb higher still into the air like a javelin. Titan arched his body back into his descent toward the city and saw the night sky light up. He could feel the intense heat against his body as the panel exploded miles above the city. His eyes never veered from the van as it continued to make its getaway.

You know, Titan, those two don't have to get away.

"I hear you, Azure. I also think I see our two little friends turning left on King Street," Titan said, rocketing back toward the city like a torpedo.

The van was still going slowly to not draw attention to itself. This only made it easier for Titan as he pulled his legs up into a cannonball position and angled himself toward the van. He could feel the force of air push against him as he neared street level. Titan punched through the roof of the van as he made contact, and crashed through the middle, practically bending it into a big white V shape. The van's front wheels continued to spin but they were no longer in contact with the road. Chunks of asphalt were kicked up as the van had been ground to a halt. Shock and Awe were both knocked around the cab of the van. Titan slowly pulled himself loose of the dilapidated van wreckage. He jumped down to the street and pulled the passenger side door right off its hinges with one hard tug.

"Well, it looks like you guys get to go back to criminal school," Titan said, pulling the two from the van.

Awe was still quite dazed, and Shock was just coming to as he put them down and began to tie them up with lengths of electrical wire from the back of the van.

"I think the police should be by to pick you two up very shortly, even on a busy night like this one," Titan said, finishing tying them.

"You've only won the battle, Titan, not the war," Shock said. He was sitting on the pavement bedside the van back to back with his sister.

"Well, I like my odds in this war," Titan replied, standing over the pair.

Titan looked around and saw that people were starting to mill about on the sidewalk, watching cautiously. Passing vehicles were staying clear, but driving past slowly with cameras or phones pressed to their windows trying to snap a clear picture of Titan, the wrecked van, and the captured super villains.

I do think it best that we leave now.

"Um, yeah I agree."

I also think it best if we call it a night.

"Sounds good. I just have one more stop I need to make," Titan replied.

Titan leaped up to the top of the tallest building on the street. He paused for a moment to get his bearings and then continued to bound his way over buildings, carefully making his way to Vicki's office. Once there he lowered himself down to her office window. It was already becoming something of a habit with them. She seemed to be adjusting her hours and working later so she could get all the latest scoops from Titan directly. He was becoming accustomed to reading about his exploits from her articles on line every morning.

"I heard about the explosions. Is everything okay?" Vicki asked, sliding the office window open.

"Yeah, mostly," Titan answered, hopping inside. He then, as quickly and accurately as he could, recounted the evenings encounter with Shock and Awe.

"That's incredible, "Vicki exclaimed. "You're lucky you didn't blow yourself up."

"Now you're starting to sound like my girlfriend." Titan suddenly paused. At the mention of any part of his personal life, he saw Vicki suddenly perk up even more than she had when she heard his story. "I mean, well, not that I have a girlfriend or anything. It's just, you know, if I did you were kinda sounding like one."

"Look, don't sweat it. I really think it's best for now if we keep this on a purely professional basis, and I know as little about you as possible." Vicki said, raising a hand to silence Titan. "You are, after all, a wanted felon. And it's not that I'm not curious. Part of the reporter in me wants nothing more than to find out more about the real you, but I also have more than I can handle just with your little superhero escapades."

"Yeah right," Titan said, he sat perched at the edge of Vicki's desk with his head down.

For a moment they both stood not talking, just looking down at the floor.

"Really, I didn't want to tell you this, especially after you've just had your neck on the line with a couple of true criminals, but the reports I am hearing is that Mr. Midnight is back. I don't know how accurate it all is so far but there are rumors. There has been a void in the criminal underworld and it looks like the real Mr. Midnight or someone taking up the mantle is back in the picture. The good news is that the police, Chief Ross in particular, are taking him seriously this time," Vicki stated, sitting on a chair against the wall. She still seemed a little hesitant and uncertain about getting too close to Titan. Not so much scared as just unsure with so much still unknown about him.

Titan hung his head. He knew deep down this news of Mr. Midnight's return would come to him at some point. He had just been hoping it not be for a while yet.

"Also," Vicki said, before Titan could even respond to her comments about Mr. Midnight. "it sounds as though you've inspired some others to put on masks and try to stop crime." She stopped and gauged Titan's look of confusion. "There are some other vigilante reports coming in over the last few weeks. I haven't said anything because I've been trying to find out as much as I could first. From what I've gathered there have been around six of these reports. At least four seem to be your run of the mill copycat stories of people that saw Titan in the news and felt inspired to do more. There are a couple, though, that are intriguing."

Titan lifted his head toward Vicki.

"They seem to have special abilities much like yourself. One report about a person made up of cloud of smoke. Another report I have is about someone that can fly and has super strength much like you."

Titan paused for a moment. He had always just assumed he would hear from Mr. Midnight again. He didn't think, however, that he would come across any more superheroes. The copycat heroes were always a possibility he supposed, but one he never gave much thought until now. He didn't want anyone innocent getting hurt thinking they could be like him. Yet, he had never imagined anyone else with superpowers. He just knew that somehow the DCPD and the Mayor's Office would blame him for anything that might happen to other citizens inspired by Titan.

"If Mr. Midnight's out there again I will find him, and hopefully sooner than later. I don't even know what to think about any other people out there with powers like me. I just hope they are on our side and not Mr. Midnight's. When you write about what happened tonight with Shock and Awe could you maybe just drop in something about me not approving of any citizens taking the law into their own hands and putting themselves in jeopardy? I know it's kind of hypocritical, but whatever."

"That sounds good, at least liability wise," Vicki said, typing rapidly on a notepad computer she had in her lap.

There was a sudden buzzing that caused Titan to jump up and grab at his belt. Vicki paused from her furious typing and glanced up at him cautiously. Titan continued to grab at his belt until the buzzing stopped, never looking Vicki's way.

"I gotta get going I guess," Titan said, making his way quickly to the open window.

"So, I guess superheroes rely on cell phones these days like the rest of us, huh," Vicki stated as Titan was half way through the window.

"Um...well you know how it is," Titan said, with a dry nervous chuckle.

Before he could say any more Vicki broke into a broad smile and waved him goodbye in a manner that said, 'don't worry about it'. Without another word Titan vanished from the window and was on top of the Courier building. He then leaped several blocks over and leaning up against a heat duct pulled his cell from his belt. It showed one missed call from Grandpa Dale. Titan opened the phone to call his grandfather back.

"Hi Grandpa, it's Michael," he said once his grandfather answered.

"Oh Michael, I'm glad I caught you," Grandpa Dale said, not knowing he had really caught his grandson in more ways than one. Titan found himself, wishing for what felt like the millionth time, that he could tell his grandfather about Titan. "I just used the last of the bread. Could you stop and pick some up before you come home? The stores will be closing soon."

"Yeah, no problem."

"Sorry to bug you on your date. I just didn't want you to find yourself short in the morning when you make your lunch."

At his grandpa's words he started to bang his head against the duct. He had forgotten about his date with Carly amidst all the commotion of the evening. He had just hung up and was just starting to run through his head what he would say to her when his phone buzzed once again with an incoming text. He clicked open the text and read Carly's message.

WHERE ARE YOU?

Titan you have done plenty tonight. You should go and be with Carly now. The probability of you being needed again this evening is quite low.

"Thanks, Azure. I really should get going to her place. I'm not sure how much she'll want to see me. I'm three hours late now."

Very well, we will speak again when Titan is needed.

"Okay, see ya later, Azure," Titan said, as he began to type his reply to Carly.

SORRY, CAUGHT UP WITH TITAN WORK!
ON MY WAY NOW.

Titan gathered his bearings and started to leap across rooftops towards Carly's building in the east end of the city. He tried to block everything out and just focus on the sounds and sights of the city as he soared over it. Street lights and buildings seem to go by in a blur of halogen streaks. The sounds of cars honking and people moving about the city all came up at him in one big muffled blast. He had become quite used to the sensation of leaping such great distances and speeding over the city, but it still sent his heart racing as he turned and arched his body where he wanted to turn and felt the wind rush past his face and pull at his body.

Only four minutes after he had said goodbye to Azure, Titan landed on the rooftop of Carly's building. If he had used any other mode of transportation the journey would have taken at least twenty minutes. Titan made his way to the rooftop doorway and said the magic words that would transform him back to Michael as he went.

"Extermino Fortis!"

Michael opened the door and descended the stairs to Carly's floor he was still drawing a blank as to what he would say to her. Part of him didn't feel he should have to say anything. He had big responsibilities as Titan, and Carly above all should be able to understand that, he thought. Michael approached the Edward's door and knocked.

Seconds later, the door swung open and Carly's father stood before him. Les Edwards didn't say anything. He simply stood in the middle of the doorway looking down at Michael with his furrowed brow and scowling face. Luckily, Michael had been getting used to the idea of Carly's father not liking him very much. The only part of it that bothered him was that he seemed to have this idea that Michael was just like his rotten, older brother, Vince.

"Hi, Mr. Edwards. Is Carly here?" Michael asked.

"My daughter seems very upset. Would you happen know anything about this?" Mr. Edwards asked, ignoring Michael's question.

"Oh, Les stop it, and let the boy in," Mrs. Edwards chimed in from behind her husband.

The scowl on Mr. Edwards face pulled even tighter as he opened the door wide and stepped aside to let Michael in. Les Edwards stood over six feet tall and was a barrel chested, broad shouldered man. Michael took his cue and entered the apartment, doing his best to keep as far from Mr. Edwards as possible.

Michael entered the apartment, Mrs. Edwards came into view. A good foot shorter than her husband, she was far less intimidating. She stood with a smile on her face as she saw him. Her hair and makeup were done in a way that indicated she was about to go out to a social gathering, even if she was only staying home for the evening.

"Carly's in her room, Michael, and yes she is rather upset at the moment. Don't worry too much about that though. You go on in and see her. I'm sure she'll be glad to see you still," Mrs. Edwards said.

"Well, hold on a minute here. I don't think I like the idea of him being in our daughter's, our fifteen year old daughter's, bedroom unsupervised," Mr. Edwards chimed in, still standing by the door, seemingly ready to toss

Michael out at any moment if required.

"I'm sure it will be all right, dear," Mrs. Edwards replied to her husband, and apparently Michael also. "Michael dear, just please make sure the bedroom door stays open, will you?"

"Um...yeah, sure thing Mrs. Edwards," Michael said, as he hesitantly stepped toward the hall and Carly's bedroom. He hated being caught in the middle of all this. Over the last few months he had tried his best to prove to Mr. Edwards that he was a good boyfriend for his daughter and indeed nothing like his older brother. Yet, nothing he did seemed to improve the situation any.

Michael made his way down the hall. He got to Carly's door, paused and took a deep breath then knocked lightly. He waited a moment then opened the door and stepped inside. He made sure to leave the door wide open as he went in.

"Hi, Carly. Look, I'm really sorry that I'm late. There was this, you know, situation that I had to deal with," Michael said, trying to tip toe around the subject of Titan as he didn't know if her parents would be able to hear him.

Carly sat at the desk in the far corner of her room, her school books and laptop open about her. Carly's room was mostly like other girls her age. She had some posters on the wall of bands and singers that she liked. There were bits of memorabilia from events she had shared with Michael or their friends. Pictures of her and Michael together were taped all over the mirror above her dresser.

"Carly, please say something. I feel terrible, really I do," Michael pleaded.

"Michael, I don't even know where to start right now," Carly said without looking up or even turning around.

"I know you're mad, but we can still go out and do something."

Finally, she stood and turned to face him. Once he glanced at her, however, he saw just how mad and upset she was.

"I've been sitting here for hours waiting to see you or even just hear from you. I've been watching web reports on my computer trying to see if there was some danger that you were caught up in. Then I hear about this explosion across town, and I just know that it has something to do with you right away. Then it's another hour before I hear from you," Carly said. Once she was done she sat at the end of her bed and put her head in her hands and let out a big sigh of exasperation.

"Carly, I am so sorry. You know I would never just leave you to worry, right? It just means I'm caught up with something," said Michael.

"It's not just that. I've hardly seen you the last couple weeks and we were supposed to have a night for just you and me for once. Couldn't you have just placed an anonymous call to the police for one night? Does it always have to be you?"

Michael said nothing to this. He started to shift his weight nervously from side to side.

"It's more than just that though. I know you have important responsibilities, but what about your school work? How are you doing with that?" she asked him looking back up to meet his eyes.

Michael said nothing to this either. He simply hung his head.

"I've kept my grades up, but lately I have been so preoccupied with focusing on you that it's been hard. Yet, I took a night off from studying and doing assignments so that we could be together." said Carly.

Michael thought of all the little things she had done to help him as Titan over the past months. Ever since she had helped him stop Mr. Midnight she had helped him do research and plan out how to capture other villains or prevent crimes that he had heard about from Vicki. It was also true that he had let his own grades slip as the school year had worn on. Now it was springtime and the slide was harder to stop so he had almost given up hope. He was not aware, though, that Carly's grades had been anything but exemplary. They had never been anything but. So, he had just assumed that she would be able to go through high school with her usual ease.

"I'm sorry, Carly. I don't know what else I can say. I was busy stopping two bad people from blowing up half the city. Yes, my grades have slipped, but I never meant for yours to as well. I'll try better to text you more often and keep you up to date, but it is hard when I'm fighting off hordes of bad guys," Michael said, his voice going into a whisper when he started to talk about Titan.

"Michael, you just don't get it. Look, I'm just too tired and I have too much homework to waste any more time on this tonight. Please, just let me get back to it," Carly said, as she started back toward her desk where her school work, her laptop was showing a page of typing Carly had been working on.

Carly sat down at her desk with her back to Michael and said no more. Michael stood there a moment, forlorn, not knowing exactly what else to say or if there was anything he could say right at that moment. Deciding it was best if he just let her cool down. Michael gingerly stepped back out of her room and closed the door gently behind him. He paused for the briefest moment outside her door. He could have sworn that he heard Carly crying on the other side.

As Michael passed through the kitchen to the front door of the apartment, Carly's parents were both sitting at the kitchen table sipping mugs of coffee. Mrs. Edwards looked up at him, eyebrows raised, as he entered. Mr. Edwards never looked up from the table.

"Everything okay then?" Mrs. Edwards asked, in that tone of hers that implied good news was really the only kind there ever was.

"Well, I don't know. She's kind of tired so I think I'll just let her rest and we'll talk in the morning," Michael replied.

"Oh, okay then. Well, goodnight. Say hi to your grandfather for us, dear, will you?"

"Sure thing Mrs. Edwards," Michael said, as he opened the door. "Goodnight."

Mrs. Edwards gave him a sympathetic little smile as he stepped into the hall and closed the door behind him. Mr. Edwards never looked in his direction the whole time. Michael never wanted to rush home faster in his life. He turned and bounded down the three flights of stairs and out the building's front door, turned left and headed for home.

Michael tried to block out everything as much as he could. He just wanted to get home and jump into bed. He was betting everything that Carly would feel completely different when she woke up and all would be well again. How could it not?

"Hey Mike!"

Michael was not even aware that he had already walked over two blocks when he heard his name called out by a familiar voice.

"Oh, hey Perminder," Michael said, as he looked back over his shoulder and saw his best friend.

"What's up, man? You just coming from Carly's?" said Perminder, with a broad smile.

"Yeah, I'm just on my way home now," Michael answered, bleakly.

"Cool, I'll walk with you. I'm just heading to Dave's," Perminder said, referring to the other member in their little trinity of best friends. "So how's Carly then?"

"Not too good at the moment, man. She's kind of mad at me 'cause I was late for a date tonight, again."

"Yeah, I figured it was something like that. You kinda had that look on your face, you know, like you're all confused and stuff," Perminder said.

The look on Michael's face must have indicated that this was not the kind of conversation that he wanted to hear.

"Sorry, man. I didn't mean to make it worse or anything."

"It's okay. I'm sure she'll feel better about it in the morning," Michael said, as they approached Dave's house.

The sight they saw ahead of them at their friend's house, however, did nothing to lighten the mood. A half block away Michael could easily make out his older brother Vince leaning against the chain link fence at the edge of Dave's family home having what seemed to be a conversation with his friend, Dave.

"Oh, I can't believe this. Mike, tell me that's not who I think it is," said Perminder.

"I'm not sure I'm seeing it myself," Michael responded.

11

The pace of the two boys slowed considerably as they saw Vince, one of their neighborhood tormentors, directly ahead. Finally, Vince looked up and noticed his little brother coming his way, and one of the most startling things he had ever seen happened. Instead of waiting to abuse Michael, Vince quickly turned and walked away.

"What was that?" Michael asked Dave, as he approached.

"Oh hey guys. That was just Vince," Dave replied.

"Yeah, my brother, but he is also the guy who has picked on, and bullied us for years," declared Michael.

"You know, he walked by and we just started talking. It was kind of weird, but once we got to really talking, I don't know, he's not that bad of a guy."

"Whoa. I think my brain just fried," Perminder said, as he stood wide eyed behind Michael.

"Look, I can't even process this right now. I gotta get going. I'll see you both tomorrow, unless you'd rather hang out with the other Novak instead," Michael said as he turned and started to walk home leaving his two best friends standing at the curb.

"Mike, it's really not such a big deal," Michael heard Dave shout from behind him.

Now Michael couldn't get home fast enough. He only hoped to avoid his older brother before he could crawl into bed. His night had been one for the books. He simply wished there was a reset button that he could hit and have a redo of the entire evening.

At last he came to the house he shared with Vince and his Grandpa. He saw no sign of Vince anywhere as he approached the back door of the house. He took this as a good sign and rushed in the door, flipping off his shoes. As he went through the kitchen and passed the living room he found Grandpa Dale sitting in his arm chair listening to the radio at his side.

"Hi, son, how'd things go?" Grandpa Dale asked.

"Well, I was late for my date, which did not impress Carly," Michael replied, as he plopped down on the couch, sparing a moment for his grandpa.

"Mad was she? Well, don't worry I'm sure she'll get over it soon. Did you remember the bread?"

Michael dropped his head into his hands. If only he could find that reset button.

CHAPTER 2: Warnings and Threats

Chief Ross sat at his desk with files and photos from three different crime scenes spread out before him. He sat for some time not moving with only his eyes darting from file to file. All three involved crimes that would have posed quite a serious threat to the general public had they not been stopped. All three had been stopped by Titan.

The police department's stance on Titan to the media was still and had always been that he was a wanted vigilante criminal. Over the last eight to nine months, since reports of Titan first appeared, the department had not come close to catching him. At least not since Inferno, the flame thrower wielding maniac, had been stopped from attacking the city by Titan. Chief Ross had many requests from the mayor's office to increase efforts to apprehend this vigilante, Titan. Yet, according to many of the latest news reports many citizens did not want him caught. There were numerous notices sent out to officers that they were to apprehend Titan on sight, but not at risk to their own safety.

Chief Ross finally stacked all the reports and pushed them aside. He pulled a new stack to the center of the desk that had been sitting on the far corner. This pile of paper contained reports from some of his detectives about Mr. Midnight and the current state of the criminal underworld in the city. It had been an interesting few months to say the least, as the power vacuum made by Mr. Midnight's apparent absence had brought many newcomers trying to take over the top spot as Delta City's criminal kingpin.

Ross then went right to the last page of the pile. On it was detailed reports of the possible return of the former mysterious crime boss. Mr. Midnight had operated for years like a phantom. The police had only developed any real information on him after he had reportedly perished at the hands of Titan. The report of his possible return was not what the chief of police needed to hear.

Ross took the new pile of papers and placed them on top of the ones about Titan. He took them all and placed them on the top rack of a tray at the corner of his desk. He was about to stand when there was a sudden and unexpected knock on the door.

"Come in."

Chief Ross stood to greet his guest. His eyes widened as Mayor Winfield opened the door and walked in. Trailing the mayor was a skinny younger man in a shirt and tie, dark thin rimmed glasses and a briefcase in hand. The mayor himself was a large potbellied man with a thick dark moustache.

"Chief Ross, may I have a word?" Mayor Winfield said, already taking a seat in front of Chief Ross. Skinny glasses just stood at attention directly behind the mayor.

"Of course, Mr. Mayor. What can I do for you?" replied Ross, sitting back down behind his desk.

"I am here to ask about the status on the police department's search for the wanted criminal vigilante known as Titan."

Chief Ross should not have been surprised to hear this as similar requests came from the mayor's office at least twice a week, but never in person.

"Well, Mayor, at this time all I can tell you is the same thing we told your office a few days ago, and that is that presently we have no leads about the identity or whereabouts of Titan."

The mayor let out a long sigh and inched forward on his chair.

"Chief Ross, why is it that every time I ask about Titan I get the same response? How can there be no new developments in this case over months and months unless the police department is simply not pursuing this criminal. Much in the same way that Mr. Midnight was not pursued actively for years while every resident of my city knew he was out there, everyone that is except the police."

Chief Ross sat forward and folded his arms across the desk. He seemed to think carefully over what he was about to say to the mayor.

"Mr. Mayor, are you suggesting that the police department let a known crime lord run his criminal business knowingly in Delta City and turned a blind eye to it?"

The mayor gave a sly smile at that, knowing he now had the police chief's undivided attention. The mayor then held up his right hand and snapped his fingers.

"Jeffery, the paper please," the mayor demanded, and skinny glasses snapped to attention and pulled a folded newspaper out of the briefcase he held.

The mayor opened the paper and placed it on the desk and slid it in front of Chief Ross. Ross leaned forward and examined the paper closely. The headline read: 'Titan Saves City From Shock and Awe.'

"Today's Courier, what am I supposed to get from this exactly?" Chief

Ross seethed, clearly annoyed.

"Do you not read these stories from this reporter?" the mayor asked.

"Sorry, I don't look for my clues in the local media."

"Well maybe you should start. It seems all her articles about Titan come right from the vigilante himself. I just wanted to show you that it seems quite obvious that someone doesn't seem to have any trouble finding this wanted man. My voters simply demand to know why the police can't also find him," the mayor said, his sly smile growing ever broader.

"If this is all, Mr. Mayor, I need to be getting back to work now," Chief Ross replied.

"Very well," the mayor said, as he started to rise. "Jeffery, let's stop bothering the chief, so he can get back to work keeping this city safe for all of our citizens."

The mayor and his assistant turned and opened the door to exit, but first the mayor stopped, and turned back for a parting word.

"Good day, Chief, and do have yourself a good day."

With that, he was gone, the door closing briskly as he left. Chief Ross sat hunched for some time over the newspaper the mayor had placed in front of him, and studied it. Shortly, he looked up and pulled the files on Titan out from the tray where he had placed them. Then, Chief Ross lifted his phone and dialed.

By mid-afternoon, Vicki Earnhardt was in her office working on her laptop. Ever since Titan had first appeared at her office window, reporting about him had become nearly a full time job of its own. She was currently working on completing her full story and interview with Titan in which he had explained what had happened with Shock and Awe. The first part of the story had been eaten up by the public, and she knew the second part would need to be in today. She had attempted to get an interview with the arrested twins, but so far had been denied by both the attorneys, and the police.

She was so focused on her story that she did not hear the light tap at her door. She only noticed when her editor, Charles, poked his head into the doorway.

"Um, Vicki, sorry to interrupt, but I have someone here who wishes to speak to you, someone from DCPD," Charles said.

"Okay, let him in, I guess," Vicki replied, not sure what someone from the police department would want with her. They had been quite clear about denying any interviews with her over the past few months in regard to Titan.

Charles opened the door all the way and entered the office. Behind him was a middle aged man in a beige trench coat with a moustache. Vicki rose to greet her guest.

"Vicki, this is detective Frank Langara of the Delta City Police

Department," Charles said, waving a hand in Det. Langara's direction.

"Please, just call me Frank," he said, as he extended and shook Vicki's hand.

"What can I do for you, Frank?" Vicki asked, as she gestured for him to take a seat. Charles simply stood, arms folded, and leaned against the wall.

"Well, we couldn't help but notice down at the station that you seem to have a direct line to the vigilante, Titan, as he calls himself. Is that correct?" Frank asked, taking his seat as did Vicki.

"I wouldn't say a direct line, but he does seem to always find me when he has something to report," Vicki said.

"You don't have a way to reach him?" Frank asked.

"No, sorry, I don't. He just shows up," Vicki replied. She started to move papers around on her desk to keep the detective from being able to see them.

"He shows up? Where does he show up, here?"

"What exactly is going on here? What is it you're trying to say exactly?" Charles asked abruptly standing upright, moving away from the wall.

"This vigilante is wanted by the police. You both realize that, right?" Frank said. They both nodded in agreement. "The department is simply following up leads as to his whereabouts and identity. You seem to be the only one to have come into direct contact with him on, what seems like, a regular basis. We just want to know if you have any way of contacting him or know anything about his identity."

"I don't. He finds me when he needs to. He just shows up, and it could be anywhere. I interview him like any reporter would try to do. He tells me his side of the story, and I report it. That's all. Even if I knew anything I couldn't say. He would be protected by me as a source. You are aware of that whole freedom of the press thing, right?" Vicki said curtly.

"I am, yes. But that only goes so far when you are harboring a known criminal," Frank said, letting out a big sigh and leaning back in his chair. "Look I'm not trying to cause a bunch of trouble for nothing. The fact is this guy is breaking the law and I need to find him before he hurts himself or others." He pulled out a business card and placed it on her desk. "If you change your mind and can give me any information it would really be appreciated."

Frank rose from the chair. He paused as Vicki stared at the card he had placed on her desk.

"The police department has not given me any help lately. I don't see why I should help you. Plus, I think Titan has been a good thing for this city. He stopped Mr. Midnight, and plenty of others. What have the police done of late besides try and stop him?" Vicki said, as she met his gaze with a distrustful glare.

Frank let out another long sigh. He didn't respond. He simply turned, waited for Charles to step aside, and left the office closing the door behind him.

By early evening Mayor Winfield was just getting back to his office at city hall. He marched up the wide front staircase of the building lobby with his assistant, Jeffery, right at his heels. They reached the top with the mayor being typically winded, and made their way down the long wide hallway to the Mayor's office.

"I still can't believe the nerve on that Chief Ross. Any real police chief would have put an end…to this Titan threat ages ago. Not him…though. He probably thinks Titan is some…great hero for the city too. That…or…he just likes that this guy is doing most of his work for him," Mayor Winfield said, as he wheezed and panted between words.

Jeffery rushed up to the Mayor's side as they made their way to the end of the hall.

"I think you gave him something to think about, Mayor," Jeffery said.

"Of course I did. That was the whole point," Mayor Winfield exclaimed. "No masked mystery man is going to run around pretending to save my city. All he does is destroy it anyway. These villains, like we had the other night too, we didn't have those before he showed up."

They reached the mayor's office, opened the door and went inside. Both men stopped abruptly as they saw what awaited them. Standing at ease by the wall, staring at some pictures of the city, was a tall broad shouldered man with a gray haired crew cut, and in full military dress. As the mayor and Jeffery entered he turned towards them.

"Mayor Winfield, I'm General Stevenson." The general walked a few paces toward the two with his hand out, like he was coaxing squirrels to eat from his palm in the park.

"What can I do for you, General?" Mayor Winfield asked, as he shuffled toward his desk.

"I'm here about a problem in your fair city," General Stevenson replied.

"What sort of problem? I mean, this is a big city, we have all sorts of problems,"

"Well, this one involves just one man. Why don't you come, sit down and I'll tell you about it?"

CHAPTER 3: Apologies

Michael walked slowly to school with his head down and his sneakers shuffling along the sidewalk. He was lost deep in his own thoughts. So much has happened in the last twelve hours that Michael had barely been able to get any sleep. After he got home that night, he had thought of texting or calling Carly several times and then stopped himself. He had no idea what he would say. Plus, he was a little nervous as to what she might say. He had never really seen her mad at him like that. Finally he had texted her before he went to bed and apologized again. He got no response. He was starting to wonder if her father, not wanting her to be with him, was starting to have an impact on her.

It had been early morning by the time he had finally drifted off to sleep. He had rolled out of bed when his alarm rang and made his way to the kitchen for breakfast. He grunted his way through a brief conversation with Grandpa Dale and then out the door to school. He was just thankful that he hadn't run into Vince before leaving.

"Hey, you just gonna leave a buddy like that?" Perminder asked, jogging to catch up to Michael.

"Sorry, man. I didn't see you," Michael said, surprised that he hadn't noticed his best friend.

"Haven't made up with Carly yet, huh?" Perminder asked.

"Is it really that obvious?"

"Well, you look a little love sick I guess."

The two boys went only about a block before they ran across Dave who was waiting for them on the corner. The three boys met this way every morning before school. Once they met Dave they would usually turn right and head toward Eastside High. Typically they would meet Carly and Monica about a block from the school as well. This morning, however, Michael had a feeling they wouldn't run into the two girls.

"Can I join you guys or is Mike still mad at me?" Dave asked once he reached them.

"Of course you can. Look, I'm sorry if I overreacted, but seeing one of my best friends being all chummy with Vince was way more than I could handle last night. I had just had a big fight with Carly." Michael deliberately left off his encounter with the murderous twins, Shock and Awe.

"Hey, don't sweat it. I can see from the look on your face that things still aren't alright in lovebird land," Dave said.

"That's what I said too, and you would be right on the mark," Perminder chimed in.

"Can we just change the subject?" Michael asked.

"Sure, you guys do the chemistry homework for last night?" Dave asked.

"Oh man!" Michael exclaimed.

"I would take that as a no from him, but I did," Perminder said.

"Uh oh, you know what Mr. Henderson is like on late assignments, and your marks aren't exactly stellar in his class so far." Dave remarked. Perminder and Dave both could see the increasing look of dread spread across Michael's face. "Look, why don't you copy down the first half of my answers, and then copy the second half of Perminder's. That way he won't know that you copied anyone's and you can get credit. What do you say, Perminder?"

"Yeah, of course, man. Mike would do the same for us. Right, Mike?" Perminder responded.

The three of them stopped at a bench at the edge of a little park, dropped their bags and pulled out their books. Michael scribbled away furiously as Dave and Perminder stood by and idly chatted, waiting for him to finish. He knew if Carly were there she would chastise him for copying his friend's work, but right now all he could think about was not failing the assignment. For once he was actually glad she was not with him.

"So, what exactly we're you talking to Vince about anyway?" Perminder asked Dave

"Please, let's not go there again," he responded.

"I'm just curious is all? How was it you were having a civil conversation with the guy. Any time I deal with him the talking is at a minimum and the whole thing usually ends with me running for my life," said Perminder.

Michael slowed his writing. He didn't want to drag the issue out with Dave, but he was curious himself about the answer to this.

"Well, I think it helped that I was standing in my own yard. It was sort of weird, but it was only a few minutes and he was just asking me what I was up to."

"Sorry man, it's more than sort of weird, but who knows, maybe Vince has changed lately. What do you think Mike?" Perminder asked.

Michael quickly finished writing, shoved his book back in his bag and handed the other books back to Dave and Perminder.

"I don't even want to know. The less time I spend thinking about my older brother the better. I get enough of him as it is," Michael finally answered. "Now, come on, we better get going before we're late for first period. And guys, thanks again for the assignment."

"No problem, buddy," Dave said slapping Michael on the back as they all turned and continued their way to school.

They weren't late. In fact they showed up with five minutes to spare. The three of them stood outside the front of the school mingling with other kids they knew. Michael, however, was quite distracted as he was keeping a watchful eye out for Carly and Monica. Finally he saw the two girls approach from half a block away. Michael stepped down hoping to meet them before they were engulfed by the throng of students at the front entrance. He noticed Carly meet his stare just as they came to the school. She quickly put her head down grabbed Monica by the elbow and darted toward the side entrance of the school. Michael barely registered as the warning bell rang signaling that all students should make their way to class.

"Come on, Mike. Let's go," Dave said, as he turned and vanished within the school's corridors.

"Don't worry. You'll see her in class," Perminder said, resting a gentle hand on Michael's shoulder and guiding him inside.

First period was chemistry. Michael was very relieved that Dave and Perminder had taken pity on him and let him copy their work as Mr. Henderson was taking no pity on students this day. He gave two students a zero as they attempted feeble excuses for not having their work complete. When Michael handed over his paper he half expected to have it thrown back in his face, and called out for plagiarizing, but somehow he was spared. When the bell rang dismissing the class, Michael let out a giant sigh of relief. Now all he had to do was get through the rest of the day unscathed.

He couldn't find Carly or Monica between first and second period. Second period was math for Michael. When the bell rang again he made his way to his third period social studies class as fast as he could. He shared the class with Perminder and Carly. The three usually sat in the back corner together. When Michael arrived Perminder was already seated in his usual spot.

"No sign of Carly just yet," Perminder said, as Michael approached and took his seat.

"What, do I really look that worried to you?" Michael said with a nervous laugh that he could clearly see Perminder wasn't buying.

"You really want me to answer that?" Perminder asked.

The class continued to fill up. Mr. O'Brian, the social studies teacher, came in and sat at his desk in the front of the room. Finally Carly came in just before the bell rang. She never even looked toward their corner. She quickly rushed in and sat in the first open desk at the front corner of the room right by Mr. O'Brian's desk. It was a desk that in eight months Michael had never seen occupied before.

Michael remained in a daze throughout the period. He was trying to devise a way to get Carly to look at him or even talk to him later between periods. Every now and again Michael would get a poke in the side from Perminder snapping him back to reality when the class would switch to opening their text books or writing something down.

Next up was lunch. In winter, Michael, Carly, Dave, Monica, and Perminder had a table in the center of the cafeteria where they would all meet. With a nice spring day like the one they had now, they would all meet in the courtyard on the grass. Michael knew he had to head her off either by her locker or in the courtyard.

When the bell sounded Michael waited until Carly gathered her things and left. He tried to stay no more than a couple of steps behind her. Once she reached her locker he finally approached.

"Hi there," he said from the other side of her open locker door. "I'm Michael, your boyfriend. I thought maybe you'd like to talk with me sometime today. Or at least look my way once in a while." He tried to hide the sarcasm in his voice, but knew he was failing. He also knew it wasn't helping.

Carly turned with her eyes already rolled up. "Are you serious? I'm mad at you, and I want you to know it, okay?"

"Oh, come on. You know how busy I am and the kind of responsibilities I have. Why are you giving me such a hard time here?"

Michael could see Carly's face suddenly contort with emotion. Her eyes welled up with tears. Her chin began to quiver.

"Michael, don't you get it. I'm thinking of breaking up with you," Carly said, holding back sobs.

Michael's eyes went wide as saucers and his jaw hung open for a moment. "What? Why? Come on, Carly, this isn't that big a deal. Let's not overreact."

"It's not all that. I just think that maybe it would be best if we just took a break. You can focus on your things and I focus on my school work. I do know how much responsibility you have, Michael, and I don't want to be a distraction for you. I can't keep staying up nights worrying about you either."

Michael stood there stunned. He had no idea what he could say or do at that moment. He had never expected Carly to say anything of the sort.

"And this won't be a distraction?" was all he could think to say.

Carly turned abruptly and headed toward the washroom with her hand held up over her face shielding her tears from the other students. Michael felt as though his feet were planted to the floor at Carly's locker. Dave and

Perminder suddenly came up from behind him.

"Okay so she just needs a little more time maybe," Perminder said.

"She wants to break up with me," Michael said. He was still wide eyed in shock.

Neither Dave nor Perminder said a word. They simply stood awkwardly at Michael's side, two silent sentries of support. At last Dave put his hand on Michael's shoulder and began to lead him away.

"Come on, buddy. Let's go and get some lunch," Dave said, as he turned in the opposite direction.

Michael suddenly pulled free of Dave and came to a complete stop. Both Perminder and Dave looked at him questioningly. The two seemed to regard Michael like some wild animal they were trying to coax into a cage. Neither said a word. They simply stood staring at Michael, waiting for him to say or do something.

"I gotta go guys. I need to find Monica before she gets to Carly," Michael said at last. The halls were bustling with the usual lunch time traffic.

Before Perminder and Dave could say a word Michael turned and began to run down the hall in the other direction. He weaved his way through the mingling students like he was once again a running back on the football field headed for the goal line. He saw many faces that he knew yet none was the one he was looking for. Monica was nowhere in sight. He racked his brain to think where she might be, but came up empty. Just as he was rounding the corner of the hall he made out a large object directly in his path. Michael was just able to shift to the side and avoid hitting it. He was not, however, able to stay on his feet and fell over onto his side.

"Mr. Novak, watch where you are going. You should know better than to be running in the halls." Michael heard the voice and knew it immediately. He turned pulling himself off the ground and saw Mrs. Samuels, the school counselor standing over him.

"I'm sorry Mrs. Samuels. I was just in a hurry to find someone," Michael said.

Mrs. Samuels wore a blue dress that hung over her short wide body like a tent. She stood glaring at Michael with two thick arms crossed over her ample bosom. Michael towered over her by close to a foot in height, yet she cast a commanding shadow. Ever since Michael had sat in her office to select his classes last spring he had done whatever he could to avoid her. Since then he had heard plenty about her from other students, none of it was very flattering.

"Is that right? Well, maybe a little detention time will slow you down a little bit." The bottom of her dress waved back and forth like the ocean as she swayed slightly, and glared at Michael.

"Oh, take it easy on the boy, Doris. Michael's a good kid. I'm sure he

23

Bankhead Library
DISCARD

isn't up to anything bad. Are you, Michael?" said a voice coming from a doorway behind Mrs. Samuels.

"No sir, Coach Walters," Michael said, looking only at Coach Walters and doing his best to avoid Mrs. Samuels.

"That is beside the point. He should know better than to run in the halls," Mrs. Samuels snapped.

Michael was just relieved that her glare had now shifted over to Coach Walters. Walters had been Michael's football coach this past fall. Michael had had a good year for a freshman, starting on special teams and doing well on the JV team. Coach Walters was wearing his typical grey sweat suit and Eastside High ball cap with a whistle hung around his neck for good measure. There was never any questioning what Coach Walters's role was in the school as one look told he was a Phys Ed teacher as well as a sports coach. This always separated him from the rest of the faculty. Coach Walters seemed to have considerably more pull within the school though than most Phys Ed teachers, and he was always ready to stand up for his players. He seemed to get away with a fair amount of favoritism to the players, but would never hesitate to pull a player from the line up if their grades were dropping.

"Well, I'm sure that Michael will be careful from here on out, won't you?" Coach Walters asked, turning back to Michael.

"Y-yes, careful," Michael stammered.

Mrs. Samuels let out a big sigh and turned to leave, the bottom of her dress fanning out wide around the bottom of her legs. She plodded off down the hall never looking back at them. Yet, somehow Michael had a feeling that she would be looking to make an example of him the first chance she got.

"Son, I suggest you tread lightly, especially around her. She does not like to be made a fool, and I won't always be there to bail you out," Coach Walters warned. "You had a good year this year; I would hate to see you ruin it by running afoul of someone like Mrs. Samuels."

"Okay, I'll be careful."

"See that you are. We'll need you next year."

Coach Walters retreated back into the class he had popped out from as quickly as he had appeared to save Michael's hide. Michael slumped forward. This day had not gone as he had planned. He figured he had long missed his opportunity to catch Monica by now. He turned and headed back the way he had come. He was in the middle of thinking what he would do next to get Carly's attention when he saw Monica step out of the girls' washroom just in front of him.

"Monica, wait up!" Michael called to her.

Monica hesitated as soon as she saw Michael. She swayed a moment as though she was going to go back into the washroom then closed her eyes a second and stood where she was and waited for Michael to approach. Michael knew that she would be rather unwilling to open up to him about Carly. He understood, and hated to put her in the middle of his and Carly's problems, but he saw no other choice.

"Monica, I just want to talk to you a second,"

"Look, Michael, I really shouldn't. I can't tell you anything about Carly so don't even ask," Monica said flatly.

"Can you just tell me exactly what it is she's so mad about?" he asked.

Monica paused a moment. Looked around cautiously then said, "Okay, look, all I can say is that it's not so much that she's mad at you. She's just confused and not sure what she should be doing."

"Confused about what?" Michael asked exasperated more at Carly than Monica.

Just then two girls came out of the washroom. They stopped abruptly, looked at Monica and Michael suspiciously and then snuck past them.

"Just give her time. When she's ready she'll come and talk to you. I mean, all she has done today is talk about you." Michael looked at her forlorn. "Don't worry," she said with a smile. "It's nothing bad, at least not too bad."

Monica reached out and gave him a pat on the shoulder and a sympathetic smile as she turned and walked away. No doubt she was off to meet Carly someplace. Michael was left standing there alone.

"Wrong door loser," a boy said as Michael stood in front of the girl's washroom.

Michael turned and headed back to meet Dave and Perminder. In the meantime he would just have to wait until Carly was ready to talk to him, and hope that time was sooner than later.

CHAPTER 4: Sonic

Michael sat forlornly at the Burger Pit after school with Dave and Perminder. A half empty basket of fries and three soda cups littered the table. Michael was vaguely participating in the idle conversation his friends were having. He hadn't seen Carly the rest of the school day. He hadn't tried to talk to her again either. He was simply allowing himself to go through the motions of an average day. Once the final bell had rung he really had only wanted to go home, but Perminder and Dave had talked him into going for some food. It was Monday and they usually hit the Burger Pit two times a week after school and often on a Monday. Michael was just grateful that he never seemed to have to work at Caruthers' Grocery on Mondays. He was not ready to have work on top of everything else.

After just under an hour they had left the Burger Pit and headed home. First Dave left and made his way home then it was Perminder, which left Michael to walk the last block and a half on his own. He enjoyed the solitude as it gave him time to think, and he had plenty to think about. He figured that if Carly was taking the time to think about their relationship then maybe he should too. He started to make a mental list of pros and cons of the two of them staying together in a romantic relationship.

There were many plus sides about them staying together, as far as he could see. He thought they were so close. They shared so many things just between them, not to mention his biggest secret which was, of course, Titan. The real thing that kept nagging at Michael was that when it was meant to be you just knew, deep down in your gut, that it was meant to be.

The con list, unfortunately, mainly revolved around Titan. Since he had accepted his role of Titan, life had been nothing short of difficult. Carly had been dragged into the whole affair simply by being there when Michael had found the ring and had first transformed. He couldn't, however, imagine if he had had to keep Titan from her as well. She would have dumped him for sure, he thought. There was always the factor that her involvement with him could place her in danger. She had, after all, been there when he had faced off against Mr. Midnight in that warehouse and the motion inhibitor. She had been fine that time but what about the future? That danger was more than he could bear to think about.

As he arrived home and opened the front gate, he paused as he heard muffled noise from inside the house. Michael broke suddenly from his reverie, however, as he realized what he was hearing was arguing. As he passed down the side of the house he could hear Vince yelling, and clearly quite angry.

"How could you tell me this now?" Vince yelled. Michael heard him easily as he passed the kitchen window.

Michael hesitated as he made his way to the back door. He was trying to assess the situation he was about to walk into. He could not hear the person Vince was arguing with, but he found it hard to believe that even Vince would talk to Grandpa Dale like that. He got to the back door and quickly opened it and stepped inside cautiously trying not to make a sound.

"Don't give me that! You are not my father!" Vince hollered from the living room.

Michael paused in the kitchen. He had never heard Vince talk like this to Grandpa Dale. Michael's instincts were to rush in and stand at his grandfather's defense. Yet, hearing Vince madder than he had ever heard before could mean pushing him to a breaking point if he tried to somehow intervene. Michael could hear Grandpa Dale say something but could not make it out. He stepped closer trying to further gauge the situation. The talking seemed to suddenly stop as Michael made the halfway point across the kitchen. Vince suddenly appeared in the living room doorway. Michael froze. Vince simply stood there glaring. His entire face seemed clenched; Michael noticed that his hands were also closed into tight fists. Michael's jaw dropped open with the intention of saying something but simply hung open with no words forthcoming.

Vince suddenly moved forward and stormed through the kitchen and out the back door without so much as a word in Michael's direction. Michael watched him go still trying to make sense of it all. He heard some rustling in the entryway and then the back door slam shut. Grandpa Dale suddenly appeared at the living room doorway. He was pale and stooped over. Michael noticed that he seemed to be putting more weight onto his cane than usual.

"Vince, please don't go," Grandpa Dale said in a low voice, seemingly knowing that Vince was long gone.

"Grandpa, what's going on? Are you okay?" Michael asked. He found the ability to speak suddenly rushing back at the sight of his grandfather.

"Michael, you're here? How long have you been here?" Grandpa Dale asked, as he reached out with one shaky hand trying to grasp the back of one of the kitchen chairs.

"I've been here long enough to hear Vince yell at you," Michael answered, as he came over and put one hand gently under Grandpa Dale's arm and guide him over to one of the kitchen chairs and helped him ease onto it.

"Don't hold it...against him, son. It's not...all his fault," Grandpa Dale said through big gasps of air.

"Grandpa, are you okay? Should I get help?" Michael asked. His anger at his older brother suddenly subsided over fear for his grandpa's health.

"I'll...be okay. I just need...the pills...in the...bottle on top of the fridge." Grandpa Dale was now slouched over and looking at the floor. Michael saw his dark glasses resting on the table, even though he could never remember a time they weren't planted on his face. Grandpa Dale ran one hand roughly through his immaculately kept hair. Seeing such uncharacteristic traits started to make Michael more nervous than anything he had yet faced as Titan.

Michael quickly went to the fridge, and with a shaky hand reached for the pill bottle on top of the center of the fridge. There were only a few pills remaining. Then he noticed the second bottle to the far right and froze, the second bottle looked slightly different, but was empty. Both bottles were labeled with Dale Novak's name and other writing that was meaningless doctor talk to Michael. The other markings on the bottles were tiny bumps that Michael recognized all too well as brail. Despite growing up with his blind grandfather, brail was the one thing he never learned to read. Michael grabbed both bottles and hoped that Grandpa Dale would be well enough to still read the bottles. He only hoped the empty bottle was meaningless and not the one they needed now.

"Here, Grandpa. There were two bottles," Michael stated, his own complexion now going a little pale.

"Thank you, son," Grandpa Dale replied, reaching out until he found Michael's outstretched hand and took both bottles.

Michael watched nervously as Grandpa Dale gently rubbed his thumb over the brail writing on one bottle and then the other. When he did so to the empty bottle he first felt along the brail and then confirming its content gave it a light shake. When it made no sound, the old man slumped forward even more in his chair, defeated.

"What is it, Grandpa?" Michael asked, already fearing that he knew the answer.

"It's empty. I could have sworn I filled it not that long ago," Grandpa Dale paused and took in a long deep breath. "It should be okay. I just need to regain my breath a little and my old ticker will slow down on its own,"

"Grandpa, if it's empty I can run out to the pharmacy and get it refilled. Or I can call an ambulance if you need," Michael said, ready to do whatever his grandfather needed. He was trying his best to block Vince from his mind.

"It's...okay...I..." Grandpa Dale said, as he broke into low mumbling that Michael could barely understand.

Michael rushed directly to his grandfather's side and rested one arm along his back rubbing it soothingly. With the other he pulled out his cell and began to text the only person he could think of that would have a calm steady head in such a situation. He scrolled down to Carly's name and began the message.

NEED YUR HELP BAD!
GRANDPA NOT WELL! COME NOW PLS!

He flipped his phone closed and looked at his grandpa. He hesitated and almost opened his phone again to call an ambulance when Grandpa Dale suddenly sat up a little straighter and began to speak. At first Michael thought he had miraculously gotten better and then realized that he was wrong and his grandpa looked as bad as ever and what he was trying to say to Michael was taking the last of his strength. Grandpa Dale had gone even paler, and his skin had started to get clammy with tiny beads of sweat visible on his forehead now.

"Michael, don't blame Vince for this. He carries too much burden as it is," Grandpa Dale said.

Michael wasn't sure at that moment who he was more angry at Vince for getting Grandpa Dale so upset or Grandpa Dale himself for trying to cut Vince some slack for Michael's sake.

"Grandpa, you don't need to defend him."

"There was something I needed to tell him. It was something I have wanted to tell you both for some time, but I wanted you to both be old enough to deal with it," Grandpa Dale said. As he spoke Michael could see the energy being drained from him as he began to slump back into his previous position as each word seemed to take longer for him to get out.

"Grandpa, don't say any more right now, just relax. I'm going to the pharmacy to get this refilled," Michael said, standing back up and making his way very slowly to the door. He just hoped that Carly would come soon and not think it as some ploy to see her.

"Michael, I need to tell you too....It's about...your parents," Grandpa Dale said.

Just then Michael heard the back door open. He rushed over to look and was relieved to see Carly there with a wide eyed worried look on her face. Monica was behind her almost cowering as though she thought there was some disease in the house she would catch.

Michael grabbed Carly by the hand and dragged her into the kitchen.

When Carly saw Grandpa Dale her mouth dropped open. The old man was now leaned back, head tilted to the ceiling, and gasping in big gulps of labored air. Monica hovered in the doorway. Michael snatched the empty pill bottle from the table.

"Please, stay with him. If it gets worse call 911 and text me. I'm going to get this refilled, it'll help him," Michael said to Carly, flashing her the empty pill bottle. Turning back to his grandfather he knelt and whispered, "Grandpa, I'm going to get your medicine. Carly is here with you. I'll be right back."

Michael turned toward Carly and mouthed the words 'thank You' to her. He reached out and gently squeezed her hand as he made his way to the back door. As he opened the door and stepped outside, he could hear Carly talking soothingly to Grandpa Dale.

Michael jogged around the house, hopped over the low chain link fence, landed on the green brown grass on the other side. Once his feet hit the sidewalk he was into a full sprint instantly. The whole way to the pharmacy the image and sound of his grandfather struggling to breath haunted him. His cell didn't chime the whole way there, which he took to be a good sign that Carly hadn't tried to contact him. The neighborhood passed by in a hazy blur as he ran. He sped through the small business area of the East end much more quickly than he was used to. It only took him four minutes to get there yet it felt closer to an hour to Michael. He burst through the front door; the bell overhead clanging loudly as he entered, and rushed passed a few other customers and familiar faces from the neighborhood as he went to the pharmacist's counter at the back of the store.

"Mr. Rodriguez, I need these refilled right away, please, for Grandpa Dale," Michael said, shoving the empty pill bottle across the counter. He was now sweaty and panting heavily himself.

"Well, let's have a look here shall we?" Mr. Rodriguez said, he seemed slightly taken a back from Michael's disheveled state. Mr. Rodriguez picked up the empty bottle, reading the script on the side. Eduardo Rodriguez was a dark haired, balding, bespectacled man in his mid-forties. He wore his white pharmacist's lab coat done up neatly as usual with three pens sticking out of the breast pocket.

"I'm sorry, son, but this particular prescription requires your grandfather to be here himself to get it refilled," Mr. Rodriguez said, sliding the bottle back across the counter.

"Mr. Rodriguez, please, he needs these pills now. Can't you just make an exception this one time? He's had a..." Michael said, pausing, not sure what exactly to call this, "an episode. Without these he will have to be taken to the hospital by ambulance for sure."

Mr. Rodriguez's brow furrowed as though in deep concentration. He glanced from Michael to the empty bottle and then back again. Michael knew that Grandpa Dale and been coming here for his prescriptions for many years and knew Mr. Rodriguez well. He only hoped that would count for something. At last Mr. Rodriguez spoke.

"I will give you a small refill order for now, but if your grandfather is truly this ill, Michael, he should be taken to the hospital anyhow." The pharmacist then reached out and took the empty bottle and scurried off to the back.

Michael waited for five agonizing minutes. He wasn't sure if he should try calling to check in just yet or not. He hadn't received a call from Carly and he did not want to jinx things just now. Finally, Mr. Rodriguez returned with the bottle now partially filled at least. Just as Michael took the bottle back from him an explosion rocked the front of the store. Glass, bits of steel and brick, and assorted merchandise went flying everywhere. The force of the blast sent Michael staggering backwards against the pharmacist's counter. Mr. Rodriguez had been knocked to the ground.

Michael could feel the force of several other explosions from farther away as the ground trembled beneath him. He got to his feet and glanced back at Mr. Rodriguez. He was also getting to his feet, his lab coat had popped open and his glasses had been knocked off. Michael grabbed under his arm and helped him get the rest of the way to his feet. He looked around the pharmacy at the damage that had been done. Michael rushed toward the front to check on the other people there. There were four others, they were all dirty, disheveled and a little bewildered. A couple had small cuts and abrasions, but no injuries appeared too serious.

Michael stepped through the hole that had moments ago been the front window of the pharmacy. A block up he saw that a car was now in smoldering ruins, as well it appeared another store front had been blown in. He could not tell which store exactly from where he was, but he was quite sure that it was not Caruthers' Grocery. Many other neighborhood residents were now coming out to see what all the commotion was about.

"Wow, man. What was that?" A familiar voice came from behind him.

Michael was relieved to see Perminder standing behind him also checking out the damage that had just occurred. Before Michael could say anything, another blast was heard farther up. When Michael turned toward it he could see a cloud of black smoke and fire that rose into the sky. Michael instinctively rubbed his ring on his right hand which also happened to be holding the re-filled pill bottle. He had never felt more torn in his whole life than this moment.

"Perminder, I need you to do me a huge favor," Michael said, turning back to his friend.

"Yeah, what do you need?" Perminder answered barely looking away from the destruction before him.

"My grandpa is sick. He needs these pills. Can you take them to him?

Carly is there waiting with him."

"Sick?" Perminder said, turning toward him. It seemed just enough to snap him out of the trance he was in. "Yeah sure. Where are you going?"

Michael put the bottle of pills into Perminder's hand and squeezed it shut. How could he possibly explain what was going on? What reason could he possibly give that would appear more important than helping his ailing grandfather?

"I have this other thing I need to do, and then I'll be right behind you," Michael said, turning toward the alley behind the pharmacy. "Tell Carly I'll be right back, but let her know that Grandpa Dale needs to go to the hospital as soon as possible."

Before Perminder could ask anything Michael had turned and was sprinting down the block. He wove through the crowd of people that had come out to check what was going on. He hit the mouth of the nearest alley and turned in. He started instantly scanning around to make sure that no other people were around to watch him transform. Michael pulled out his cell, flipped it open and began to text Carly. He knew she would be upset with him, but he saw no other way. He simply could not risk being with his grandfather at the expense of the lives of others. Whoever was setting these explosions, he knew it was Titan's responsibility to stop, and make sure that no one got hurt. He had made sure that Grandpa Dale was in good hands, so, now he had to attend to other business. However, these thoughts did not entirely wipe out the guilt that Michael was feeling.

> PERMINDER IS COMING WITH MEDS.
> GRANDPA WILL NEED TO GO TO HOSPITAL.
> I WILL BE THERE AS SOON AS I CAN. KEEP ME POSTED.

Michael hit send and set his phone down on the hood of a car parked in the alley. He then raised his arm high overhead and said the magic words.

"Exaudio Fortis!"

The magical blue lightning crashed into him with sudden force. Michael barely even blinked when it struck, as he was hardly fazed by the occurrence any longer. With wisps of smoke still circling around his feet he quickly grabbed his phone tucked it into his belt, and leaped to the top of the building. From there he had turned toward where the last explosion had come from. He coiled his legs and launched himself into the air so he could scan below for who was responsible.

"Azure, it looks like we may have our old friends Shock and Awe back to their old tricks already," Titan said, as he was seeing the smoke and fire from the explosions as they wove a trail of destruction that now lead deep into the city.

This seems much more randomly destructive than their usual pattern. You best be weary as you approach until we know what you are facing.

"I have to find the source first. All I see now is smoke and fire."

Just as Titan landed on a rooftop about sixteen blocks away from the pharmacy a new explosion rocked the city. Titan quickly glanced that way and saw a new column of smoke rise into the air. He instantly leaped into the air and headed straight for it. He kept his gaze on his target ahead, and refused to look directly down. He could hear the sound of approaching fire and police vehicles moving toward the blast behind him.

He cautiously landed in the street at the most recent explosion, body tensed and ready to act. He felt the heat of it ripple out, engulfing him. It was easily the biggest explosion so far. He found he was at the foot of midtown in front of city hall. Smoke was still rising high into the air from the blast. Chunks of concrete and other assorted debris littered the ground all over the area. It seemed that the explosion was right in the front of city hall, but with so much smoke, Titan had a hard time seeing just how much damage was done, or how many were injured.

Just then Titan felt a giant gust of wind and something hit him hard in the stomach. He doubled over slightly, gasping for air. He felt something round and hard against his stomach as he clutched it with both hands. When he looked down he saw that he held a thin flat disc that had glowing green lights along it. It was also beeping.

Just as Titan realized what it was and was about to toss it high into the air, the bomb exploded in his hands. It sent him flying backwards. He landed hard on the hood of a car that had been deserted in the middle of the street. He felt stunned as he crawled out of the caved in hood and tried to stand. The world around him shifted and swayed as he waited to get his bearings back. He looked down at himself. His gloves and shirt were shredded, and trickles of blood ran down his stomach and over his hands. Once again he was very thankful for his super strength and durability.

As Titan staggered in the street, another gust of wind rushed straight at him like a speeding train. The speeding object stopped suddenly a few feet away, and a strange man was standing oddly before him. The man was wearing dark green armor on his torso and arms. There was a pack on his back and a dispenser on his hip. He pushed a button on the dispenser and another disc popped into his hand. He had a dark green helmet and tinted goggles. A giant glowing green letter M was on his belt buckle. When Titan looked down at the man's legs he knew then why the man stood so strangely. His legs were robotic, and like nothing he had ever seen before. Powerful springs and pistons hissed as the man stood before Titan. The legs, Titan thought, looked as much like the workings of a fast motorcycle as anything else.

"You don't wear his symbol. You won't stop me. You can't!" the man said rather anxiously.

"What are you talking about? Who's symbol?" Titan questioned, still regaining his strength.

"He calls me Sonic, and if I don't do what he says he'll take my new legs away." Sonic then tossed the disc in his hands at Titan and vanished in a blur.

If his arms had been as fast as his legs Titan would not have had time to pull out his staff and bat the disc high into the air where it exploded harmlessly. He looked around and saw no more sign of the mysterious Sonic.

"I don't know what that was even about," Titan said to Azure.

He is clearly working for someone else. He seems quite terrified of that someone.

"Yeah, and he seems beyond reasoning with right now," Titan said while still scanning the area for signs of Sonic.

Titan felt that familiar gust of wind, and out of nowhere a fist suddenly slugged him in the jaw. It dropped him to his knee. Titan quickly looked up and saw Sonic.

"Sonic, don't do this..." Before Titan could say anymore Sonic vanished again in a blur.

Titan got to his feet. As soon as he did he felt blows all around his body. Only a green streak was visible around him. Blow after blow erupted around his chest, head and back. Once the barrage stopped Sonic was again standing before him. He hit the button on his waist four times and quickly dropped four discs into his hand. Then he was gone in a streak once again. Titan could hear the beeps of the tiny discs and could only flip backwards as high and fast as he could to avoid the attack. The discs suddenly landed and exploded in a fiery blast right where Titan had been standing.

Titan stood staring at Sonic who was about twenty feet away. Sonic seemed to be nervous and jittery, but Titan got the impression it wasn't him that was making him nervous. Just as the two stood in an old west styled standoff Titan heard a loud rumble and the ground began to tremble slightly. Just then, to his right, a tank rolled into view blocking the street exit. To his left came another rumble and an army jeep armed with troops carrying large machine guns blocked the exit on the other side. With another loud approach Titan turned and saw that another jeep, this one equipped with a rocket launcher on top, blocked the last exit behind him. Sonic barely seemed to register this new development, and still did not move. As Titan gazed back at the tank, the hatch opened and a man with gray hair and moustache popped out of the opening. He seemed to be actively joining the standoff, and gazed at Titan and Sonic in front of him.

"BOTH OF YOU, STAND DOWN NOW!" commanded the man on top of the tank, as he bellowed into a mike.

Titan I think it best that you vacate these premises and let the military handle this situation from here.

"I think you may be right there, Azure," Titan said under his breath.

Titan cast a quick glanced at Sonic. He was astonished to see him hit the button on his hip several times and catch four discs as they popped out blinking. The tank turned its gun directly at Sonic, as did the rocket launcher jeep, and the armed men on the third army vehicle. Titan clutched his staff tighter as he waited for something to happen.

Sonic vanished in a flash and an explosion erupted at the base of the tank, kicking up big chunks of the street as it did. A second later, another explosion went off by the rocket launcher. Suddenly, a series of explosions detonated around the street and the military vehicles. One of the jeeps was knocked on its side with soldiers sent flying, while the glass was blown right out of the lower floors of a nearby building.

On instinct Titan leaped toward the jeep loaded with soldiers just as a final explosion erupted. He dropped to the left of the jeep and shot his staff out, hoping beyond hope that he had aimed well. A sudden force hit the end of his staff, and Titan watched as Sonic suddenly came into focus and went soaring through the air. The force of Sonic colliding with the staff made Titan stagger. He had no idea how fast Sonic had been moving but the force of impact gave him a rough idea.

Sonic skidded across the large intersection of the city. Sparks shot out all around the metal of his legs. Titan could see him trying to maneuver himself around so that he could get back to his feet. Titan could not let that happen. He leaped swiftly to where Sonic had ground to a halt, face down and was struggling to his feet. Titan stood over him, staff in hand, straddling him as best he could, and aimed the end of his staff at Sonic's head.

"Don't move," Titan seethed at Sonic.

"No! I must complete my mission," said Sonic, more to himself than to Titan.

"What Mission?" Before Titan could get an answer the loudspeaker from the tank bellowed to life again as the tank began to roll toward them slowly.

"DO NOT MOVE OR WE WILL ENGAGE!" the voice came on the other end. To prove his threat was not just mere words the cannon on the tank began to swivel and turn until it aimed directly at them.

Titan, I think we should immobilize this foe and take our leave before matters get much worse.

"On it," Titan said as he quickly jabbed his staff out and clubbed Sonic across the shoulder blades with it. Sonic dropped to his knees momentarily and then tried to climb back to his feet. Titan brought his staff down on the top of his head this time, and saw his helmet crack from the blow. Sonic went limp and tumbled to his stomach, unconscious.

Titan slowly rose until he was standing and facing the tank. He glanced around and saw that the soldiers from the other two vehicles were regrouping. The cannon was still aimed at him. He very slowly took three big strides to his right. The cannon did not move to follow him. Titan was puzzled but greatly relieved to say the least. Sonic was very fast but Titan was rather quick himself. He figured that he just may be faster than the swivel arm of the tank cannon. He bent, coiling his legs slightly, and then launched high into the air toward the east end.

When he heard no return cannon fire he was relieved, but still puzzled. He landed on a skyscraper roof just fifteen blocks from his neighborhood. He glanced back toward city hall and could see the haze of black smoke still billowing from the street.

"What was that all about?" Titan asked himself, rubbing his side which was bruised and tender with scrapes, cuts, and bruises.

Suddenly he heard a great deal of electric static come from the street below. Titan went to the rooftop ledge and looked down. Many people on the streets below had covered their ears against the static screeches, and were looking around for the source of the noise.

A giant video billboard hung off one the downtown skyscrapers and looked over the busy section of Queen St. where a multitude of shoppers were roaming the sidewalks. The screen was showing a commercial for cola as static lines rolled over the screen, and a voice suddenly cut through the static. Many other video screens and signs that hung in the area were also being overridden with the same static and noise. Suddenly the cola images were replaced by a dark silhouette of a man's upper body. As the shadowy person began to speak all activity on the street came to a standstill.

"Good day citizens of Delta City," said the shadowy man. "For too long this city has stood as a bastion of hope to many around the world for peace and equality. Even though that peace came at the price of the lives of others in different parts of the world and that equality was nothing but smoke and mirrors. Today I have come with my own small but effective army to show the people of Delta City that they are no more safe than those innocents abroad. Sonic, with his heightened speed and explosive attack, is but the first of my little creations that will be unleashed upon this city. More will come until Delta City is but ashes."

The screen then went back to showing commercials; this one was about a new car. The people on the street seemed quite bewildered and began to look around. Titan even heard a couple of squeals of panic from the crowd. Then pandemonium started to set in as people began to flee as fast as they could. There were no more explosions at that moment to cause full panic, but the fear of the promise the shadowy man had made was enough, and no one wanted to be around if those promises came true.

"Okay, so we seem to have bigger issues here than Sonic," Titan said, stepping back from the ledge.

Clearly yes, there is something bigger going on here. Sonic seemed quite frightened of this man on the screen. It appears that this man built those legs for him, as well as his weaponry. Who knows what else waits to attack.

"Yeah, and those military guys were a little unexpected as well. I thought the mayor maybe called in the army to take me out," Titan said, sitting wearily on the building's ledge.

Yet, the armored vehicle made no move toward you as you left. It seems they were not here for you at all. We do not know if they were here for Sonic either. It could easily be for the one who created him as well. I do think it wise that we find this person before the army does. Perhaps we should pay a visit to the reporter now.

"I agree with you, Azure, but we'll see about tomorrow. My grandpa is not well, and I really need to be getting back to him," Titan said, slowly getting back to his feet. "As soon as I know he's okay I'll go and meet with Vicki, I promise."

Very well. But we will hear from this individual again and we know not when. He will no doubt send more agents to attack the city. We must find out who he is and what his motives are as soon as we can.

"I'll track him down as soon as possible, honestly."

Titan faced east, got his bearings and leaped into the air toward home. He landed in the alley behind his house. Most of the fences facing the alley were high and boarded. With a quick glance to make sure that there were no others present to witness his transformation he said the magic words aloud.

"Extermino Fortis!"

Back in his own clothes Michael burst through the back gate and ran to the house. He went in the back door and found himself staring into an empty kitchen.

"Hello! Hello?" he called out. No reply came.

He spotted a yellow sheet of the kitchen paper in the middle of the table. He picked it up and read it hastily.

Michael,
Perminder came with the pills. Grandpa Dale didn't improve. We
called an ambulance and they took your grandpa to Delta City
General. We all followed and will wait for you there.
                                                    Carly

Michael stared at the note a moment without moving. So many thoughts were racing through his mind he found it hard to pin down just one and focus on it. He had to get to the hospital right away and find out how Grandpa Dale was doing. That was the only thing he was sure of currently. He glanced at the ring and debated about transforming to make the easy leap there in seconds, but thought better of it. Azure had made it quite clear there would be no tolerating using the ring for any personal reasons.

The hospital was about a fifteen minute drive by car from where Michael lived. It took him twenty-five minutes and two buses to get there. The Delta City General Hospital was a monstrous old gothic building right at the edge of East and West Delta City. The bus stopped right in front of the main hospital entrance and he dashed off and raced through the main doors. He went straight to the main information desk to find out where his grandpa was.

"Hmmm...it doesn't seem that any Dale Novak is in our system," said the bespectacled woman working at the desk as she typed away furiously at a computer.

"Are you sure? He should have been brought in a couple hours ago," Michael said, wringing his hands together nervously.

"Oh, wait, here he is. Fourth floor cardiac wing room 412A," the receptionist said without looking up at Michael.

Michael darted to the large bank of elevators, which were currently deserted, and hit the up button. One of the seven sets of doors instantly opened and Michael entered and hit four. The door closed half way and then suddenly opened again as a group of people began to filter into the elevator. It began to close again but opened just about an inch from closing all the way, and another man stepped inside. Michael was now pushed into the back corner of the full car. Not even this, it seemed, could go quickly for him.

Once the elevator chimed at four and the doors opened Michael had to fight his way out before the doors closed again. A sign on the opposite wall said 'CARDIAC' and pointed to his right. Michael followed it. As soon as he got to the waiting area Michael saw Carly, Monica, and Perminder.

"Michael!" Carly practically squealed as she spotted him, and ran toward him, arms outstretched.

As her arms wrapped around him tightly he suddenly thought that nothing had ever felt so good and comforting in his life.

"How is he?" Michael asked.

"He's stable. That's about all they'd tell us since we weren't family members. We just wanted to wait for you to get here," Carly answered.

Michael's heart began to beat faster as he noticed Carly was still clinging tightly to his left hand. Perminder and Monica gaped at him as though they were waiting this whole time for Michael to come and say something that would make it all better.

"Thanks you guys. I really mean it. I don't know what I would have done without you guys stepping up for me today," Michael said at last.

"No problem buddy," Perminder said.

"Yeah, we're just glad we could help," said Monica.

"We were mostly just waiting after we got him here, but then at least we had another Titan exploit to keep us entertained." Perminder gestured to the waiting room TV mounted high on the wall behind them that still seemed to be showing a series of clips from his battle with Sonic. "Not sure if you heard, but this time he got into a rumble with this joker outside city hall and the army actually showed up. It was crazy, man."

"Yeah, I kinda caught glimpses of it," Michael replied.

"It's just too bad the guy escaped after Titan left, 'cause he had that guy beat but good," Perminder said enthusiastically.

"What do you mean escaped?" Michael asked.

"You didn't hear that part?" Perminder asked. "Yeah, after they had him piled in some armored truck, it was attacked. Someone blew a hole in the road and ripped the guy right out of there from underground. Cops have found nothing but dead ends in the sewers apparently."

"Look, I think that's enough. Michael should probably be getting in there," Carly interrupted, seeing the look of defeat on Michael's face.

"Yeah, I guess I should really get in there and check on things."

"Look, call me whenever you get a chance and let me know what's happening, okay." Carly said, letting go of his hand.

Michael tried to smile the best he could and nodded his head. Then he went through the double doors leaving his friends behind. He turned right and followed the curve of the wing until he came to room 412A. Michael hesitated a moment, took a small breath and then walked into the room.

It was a single room with only Grandpa Dale in it. Grandpa Dale was lying in his bed fast asleep with a number of cords connected to him. Several came from the top of his hospital gown to a monitor that seemed to be reading his heart. Another was a breathing tube connected to his nose. There was also an IV coming from his arm to a bag of clear fluid attached to the top of a pole beside the bed.

Michael walked over, stood next to his grandfather and rested his hand gently on his arm. He watched intently as his chest hitched and rose with each gasp of air he took. He heard a noise behind him and saw a nurse enter the room.

"Oh, you must be his grandson. He was asking for you," the nurse said.

"I am. Is he going to be okay?" Michael asked.

"Hard to say right now, he's had a heart attack. At the moment he's stable, so that's good. We'll know the extent of the damage to his heart over the next few days. Right now we have him slightly sedated so that he can sleep."

"Can I sit with him for a while?"

"Of course, here's a chair." The nurse pulled a hard plastic chair from the corner and brought it over to him. "Just remember that visiting hours end at eight. Okay, Vince?"

Michael winced at the sound of Vince's name. He didn't bother to correct her. He didn't want her to think that he was the unwanted or the less favored one. The nurse left and Michael sat alone for the next few hours watching his grandfather sleep, and wondering what the conversation had been between Grandpa Dale and Vince, that had led to all this.

CHAPTER 5: Vince

"I sure am sorry to hear about your grandpa, son," said Mr. Caruthers. "I've always greatly respected the man and that's not something I can say about many in this neighborhood. You take the next couple of days off if you need. This is no time to be worrying about this old place."

"Thanks, Mr. Caruthers," Michael replied.

They stood at the front of the store which just happened to be, thankfully, deserted. Michael had spent much of the previous evening at the hospital. He had left only when the nurse had come to tell him that visiting hours had ended. He had made his way home by bus and by foot partly in a daze. He hadn't even noticed how much his body ached form his battle with Sonic until he had walked the last few blocks home and his whole body screamed with strained and bruised muscles. After a night's sleep he decided he wasn't going to school that day or to work either. School was easy; he just wasn't going to show up. Work on the other hand was not. He knew he would have to stop and tell Mr. Caruthers what had happened to Grandpa Dale. Michael was slightly surprised to see such shock and concern on the old shop keeper's face as he listened to Michael.

"You just be sure to give you old granddad my best. You just be ready to come back to work once he gets better, okay."

"Thanks for understanding, Mr. Caruthers. I should know some more about how he's doing today. I'll keep you posted, and I'll be sure to give him your regards."

Michael then left the store and made his way to the bus that would take him to the hospital. As he walked he was once again grateful for the accelerated healing of the ring, as his muscles no longer ached. A million other thoughts raced through his mind as he walked, however. So much had happened over the last couple days, even by Michael's standards. He had nearly been blown up as Titan twice. He had had a run in with the army. He had also nearly lost his grandfather. Plus, he had no idea where his brother was; Vince had not come home all night. Michael couldn't say he was too upset about that one, however. He still didn't know how he would act toward his brother when he saw him. Then on top of it all he had nearly been dumped by Carly.

He had finally called her once he had gotten home the night before. He had actually been a little nervous to call, as one more piece of bad news would have been one piece too many. Yet, over all, the conversation had seemed much like old times to Michael.

"How is he?" she had asked.

"Okay, I guess. He was sleeping the whole time. The nurses kept reassuring me and saying that he was stable. I should be seeing the doctor tomorrow," Michael answered.

"Well, that's good. Just stay positive, you know," Carly said, as reassuringly as she could.

"Carly, I just wanted to say thanks. I think he may still be alive because you were there to look after him," He had told her.

"Michael, you don't have to thank me. I'm only glad I could help."

"I wasn't sure you'd come after all that had been going on between us," Michael said.

"You should know that no matter what; I'll always be there for you," Carly responded.

"Well, I just wanted to thank you. It was so hard going in to face Sonic knowing that Grandpa Dale was so sick, but I knew he was at least in good hands with you."

"You did what you had to, and I had your back. That, I guess, is the way it should be." Carly declared.

"Does that mean that you're not going to break up with me?" He had asked.

"It was rather silly of me to question it in the first place, don't ya think?" Carly asked in return.

"No. Carly, I know how hard having something like Titan in our lives is to deal with. Having you there, though, is what gets me through it. I may have other responsibilities, but you have to know how much you mean to me. I love you."

"I love you too."

In the end it had been that simple, and they were back together. It had at least made facing a day of great uncertainty that much easier. Carly had even agreed to meet him at the hospital after school. Michael would be counting down the hours until he had her there for support.

At last the bus he had taken pulled up to the front of the hospital. Michal got out and made his way inside. This time he went straight to the elevator, knowing exactly where Grandpa Dale's room was.

"Michael?" Grandpa Dale asked, his head turned toward the door, but not quite facing it.

"Yeah, it's me, Grandpa," Michael called out.

"I thought I recognized your footsteps. This place still has me a little off kilter though," Grandpa Dale replied.

Michael was surprised to see that Grandpa Dale still had a tired look on his face despite all the sleep he had had after arriving at the hospital. He also had a five o'clock shadow and an uncharacteristically messy head of hair that resembled a grayer version of Michael's than the usually immaculately combed hair of Dale Novak.

"How are you feeling?" Michael asked, taking the chair he had the day before and pulling it closer to the bed before sitting.

"Oh, I'm still quite weak and I really don't know how I can be feeling so tired, but other than that I suppose I shouldn't complain," Grandpa Dale responded.

"Well, that's good then. You're still in here to make sure you get the rest you need, so don't feel bad about it, just take it."

Grandpa Dale smiled slightly and nodded his head.

"Michael," Grandpa Dale said. He paused and looked at Michael. A look of calm reflection crossed his face. It was the kind of look that Michael usually saw when Grandpa Dale was deep into some story regarding Michael's parents or especially his grandmother, Emma.

"I want to thank you, son. I am so grateful that you were there and knew what to do. If not for you I may not be here right now, and I cannot forget that." He then reached out, his hand searching for Michael's. Michael's hand wrapped around the groping hand of his grandpa.

"Grandpa, you don't have to thank me. I'm just glad I was there when I was. Plus, Carly, Monica, and Perminder did just as much if not more."

"I know and I will thank them in due course, but it's you, son, who is the one they acted upon. You are a born leader like your father, Michael. You get people to act."

Michael lowered his head bashfully despite the fact that Grandpa Dale couldn't see him. Michael sat silently, not knowing what he could possibly say. At last Grandpa Dale once again broke the silence.

"Michael, I do want to tell you what I told Vince. I hope it does not upset you the way it did him. You should know as well, though."

Michael suddenly sat upright. His chest tightened at hearing his grandfather mention Vince like that.

"Grandpa, please don't defend him. He doesn't deserve it he..." Michael caught himself before he was able to get too worked up. The last thing he wanted was to get his grandpa upset while he was still so weak.

"Son, don't blame your brother. Try to see things from his point of view. Maybe he had a right to get upset with me."

"I doubt that. I heard the way he spoke to you."

"Michael, you don't even know what I'm going to say yet. It may upset you as well."

Before Michael had a chance to contemplate this, a nurse and doctor came into the room.

"Hello, Mr. Novak. How are you feeling today?" said the doctor, as he walked toward the bed while looking down at the chart in his hands.

"Not too bad, Dr. Lieu, I think I'll be fit to go home pretty soon," Grandpa Dale replied, breaking into a broad smile.

The doctor smiled as he looked up at Grandpa Dale. He tucked his chart under his arm and approached the bed. The nurse stood a step behind the doctor the entire time.

"I'll take your assessment under advisement." Dr. Lieu chuckled. "Unfortunately you'll have to let me decide that, okay?"

"Dr. Lieu, I'd like you to meet my grandson, Michael. "

"Hi," Michael said, as he smiled and nodded toward the doctor.

"Good day, Michael. I'm sorry, but you may want to leave the room as the nurse and I have some tests we need to run on your grandfather. You can come back in once we're all done. Probably in about 20 minutes," Dr. Lieu said, as he was now holding Grandpa Dale's arm by the wrist and looking at his watch.

"Um, yeah sure, no problem," said Michael, as he stood from his chair. "Okay, I guess I'll be back in a bit, Grandpa."

Michael left the room and headed back toward the big bank of elevators. From there he had no idea what else to do so he made his way down to the cafeteria and gift shop area on the main level. So many thoughts were swirling in his head though that he could not even start to think about eating anything. He even went into the gift shop and thought of buying a magazine or comic book, but he wasn't in the mood to focus on any of those either. All he could think about was what Grandpa Dale could possibly have to say to him that could have such an impact.

At last he went outside to the front of the hospital. The only thing he could really think of doing now was to call Carly. He pulled out his cell and dialed. The phone rang several times and then went to voice mail. Then he looked at his watch and realized that she would be in the middle of her English class. He closed his phone and tucked it away without leaving a message. After wandering around the lower level of the hospital a little longer Michael made his way back up to his grandpa's room.

Michael was lost in his own thoughts as he exited the elevator and walked down the hall to Grandpa Dale's room. He suddenly crashed back down to reality however, when he collided with someone coming back through the doorway to his room.

"Oh sorry..." Michael said, assuming it to be Dr. Lieu.

"You better be sorry, jerk," seethed Vince as he looked down at

Michael, his brow crinkled in anger and disgust.

"You've got a lot of nerve showing up here," Michael snapped, almost without thinking, his emotions instantly taking over.

Michael saw Vince's hands draw into tightly clenched fists. Vince's lips pulled tighter until his mouth was barely visible at all. The two brothers simply glared at each other as hospital visitors and staff passed by all around them. Michael could practically hear his own heart pounding.

"This isn't the time or the place, loser," Vince hissed. "Now, outta my way!"

Vince pushed past Michael slamming his right shoulder into Michael's. It was hard enough to send Michael back a good step. Michael watched as Vince walked to the elevators, never once looking back.

He didn't know what bothered him more, the fact that Vince had shown up, the fact that he had slammed into him or that Vince had been the one to take the high road and not let anything ensue. Michael was a little ashamed that he had let his emotions get the better of him. After so long, he had finally tried to stand up to his brother, and he had done so in a busy hospital with his ailing grandfather not more than fifteen feet away. He hated just letting Vince walk away like that.

"So you ran into your brother," Grandpa Dale said as Michael at last entered the room.

"Um...yeah, sorry, Grandpa," Michael replied standing at his grandfather bedside.

"It's alright, son. Just don't be so hard on him."

"I know, it's just sometimes he's just so selfish and..." Michael caught himself before he started to get rolling. "Sorry, I don't want to upset you."

"Michael, I know you blame him for me being in here, but don't. It wasn't his fault. You both need to get along right now. I need you both until I can get out of here."

"I know. So, tell me, what did the doctor say?" asked Michael, trying to change the subject.

"Well, he thinks I'll be in here for the rest of the week. They want to run some tests and do something called an angiogram."

Michael was trying to listen and be attentive, but all he could think about was Vince. Why had he even bothered to show up? Where had he been until now? Where was he going? All these thoughts were swirling around his head until he simply couldn't take it anymore.

"You know, Grandpa, you look a little tired. Maybe you should just get some rest. You know I have some errands I have to run anyway." Michael said.

"I am a little tired I suppose, but I don't want you to have to leave. After all you came all this way just to visit."

"Don't you worry about me. You know that the doctor said you need to get what rest you can right now. Look, I'll be back this evening and we can have dinner together."

Michael moved in and gave him a loving kiss on the top of his head. Before Grandpa Dale had a chance to respond, Michael was moving toward the door.

"Well, if you really don't mind. I guess it is high time I start obeying doctor's orders."

"Okay then, see you soon, Grandpa," Michael said, as he left the room.

Michael was moving fast now. He had to catch Vince if he was going to have some of these questions answered. He knew he should be spending time with his grandpa, but he also felt he had to watch out for his brother. He knew deep down Grandpa Dale was right, and that maybe he shouldn't blame Vince for things. He also knew that if Vince had fallen in with bad people again that he had an obligation to watch out for him. As he wove his way through the hall he pushed all his anger about Vince as far away as he could, and tried to focus on simply getting some answers. There was only one way he could think of to get those and that was to simply find out what Vince was up to once and for all.

Michael stopped when he saw the group of people waiting for the elevator. He decided not to wait and instead took the door leading to the stairs. He bounded down the steps two at a time. Once he hit the main level he flew through the door and entered the lobby. He scanned the busy foyer, but saw Vince nowhere. He forced himself to slow down, went through the main door and stepped outside. Thankfully Vince was quite tall, and usually stood out in crowds. Finally, Michael could see the back of his head moving down the sidewalk toward the bus stop. Michael started to follow, being careful to stay a little way back and out of sight.

Michael expected Vince to stop and wait at the bus stop, but to his surprise Vince didn't stop. He walked right past the throng waiting for the number four and just kept walking. Michael found it hard to believe that Vince would walk all this way from the east end. Could he have found a ride?

Michael stayed back as he continued to follow but it became harder as Vince passed most of the crowds making their way to and from the hospital. Michael was just hoping that Vince wouldn't look back and see him but the rest of the world seemed to be the last thing on Vince's mind as he walked on with his head down and his feet shuffling along the sidewalk.

At last Vince turned a corner a block away and he came up to an old car parked in front of a meter. Michael hung back and poked his head around the corner watching intently. Vince snatched a parking ticket off the windshield crumpled it up and opened the driver's door and got in. Within seconds the engine roared to life and Vince was driving away.

"Where on earth did Vince get a car?" Michael said to himself under his breath.

With the car speeding away Michael didn't know what to do. Suddenly he glanced down at the ring. With a quick glance around to make sure he wasn't seen, he said the words.

"Exaudio Fortis!"

Before the smoke had even cleared Titan had leaped to the nearest rooftop and began to follow parallel with Vince's car. The car was an old maroon Olds and easy to spot from up high. There were plenty of buildings tall enough for him to hide among so he could avoid being spotted by Vince.

Titan what is going on? Is there some crime I am not aware of?

"Well, I'm pursuing someone who I believe to have links to the criminal world," Titan replied to Azure.

It was not a total lie. This was Vince after all. Titan was worried what Azure would think of this little mission. He was also starting to worry what he may actually find Vince doing.

What crimes do you believe they are responsible for?

"That's just it, I'm not entirely sure," Titan said, as he took a jump to his left crossing over busy sixth avenue. Suddenly he realized that Vince was currently headed toward the docks.

So, we are pursuing this...

"Okay, it's Vince. It's my brother, Vince, that we're following," Titan said curtly. He couldn't avoid telling Azure any longer as his attention was needed on his path ahead.

I see. You should have simply informed me of this development.

"I didn't think you'd understand. He's my brother, and I know he's up to no good. I know he was at that bank heist when I first went out as Titan, and we found him poking around the warehouse where Mr. Midnight just happened to be bringing his mass motion inhibitor," Titan told Azure, feeling relieved to finally say it all out loud. "I just have to know more of what he's up to."

I do understand, and you are probably doing what is best. You needn't fear telling me such information, Titan. Your brother is someone we know, at the very least, to associate with undesirables, and it makes sense that we learn who exactly those people are and make sure he is not up to worse. Your relationship to him of course makes this a delicate matter. If we find anything about your brother that is truly troubling then we shall discuss how to handle the matter further.

"Okay, Azure. It may be nothing, but I just have to know. Thanks for understanding."

That is what my duty is. I am charged to help all Titans understand not just how to handle their powers but also how to handle the difficult situations that they will face.

As they got closer to the docks the buildings grew gradually lower with less coverage, and it became harder for Titan to stay out of sight. He dropped lower and tried to stay as out of sight and concealed as possible. The Olds wove its way through the docks which were largely deserted even at this early point of the day. Many of the buildings closer to the docks were boarded up and looked to have been empty for some time.

Finally Vince parked the Olds in front of a two story office at the edge of the water. Here many dock workers milled about. Titan found a large stack of metal shipping containers and managed to find a shadowy spot that he could hide in, but still clearly see Vince and the Olds. Vince got out and nodded to a few people walking past. Someone on a forklift honked and came roaring up just to say hi to him. Vince had clearly been around enough to be familiar with the people who worked here. Yet, Vince had never said anything about working at the docks. Before Vince could reach the door to the office, Dylan Thompson suddenly came out dressed in a suit. The suit made him look incredibly out of place in a blue collar area such as this, but Dylan looked right at home to Titan.

Dylan had taken a step forward and stopped and waited for Vince to rush up and greet him. The two shook hands and then spoke briefly to each other. Titan could only assume it was small talk as they both appeared to be smiling and laughing, which was a stark contrast from the dour looking Vince he had met at the hospital.

Vince then reached into his jacket and pulled out a small manila envelope and handed it to Dylan. Dylan opened and examined it, but pulled nothing out of it. After he had peeked inside he smiled, which gave Titan an unsettling feeling. Dylan then pulled out a thick brick like package wrapped in white paper and gave it over to Vince. Vince took it and the two continued to exchange words. There was no longer any laughter between them. Titan wished more than anything that he could hear what they were saying.

They shook hands again and Dylan retreated back into the building. Vince hesitated a moment and then climbed back into the Olds, backed out and pulled away in the same direction he had come from. Titan leaped from his cover and continued to follow the Olds as it wove its way back through the city and toward the east end. As the city stretched on it began to regain its familiarity as they got closer to the east end that had been their home for so many years. Before they entered their neighborhood though, Vince made a turn and began driving back in the other direction again. Titan continued to follow and stay low and a little back from the Olds.

Finally the Olds pulled up in a residential neighborhood and parked at the curb. Titan had been following, but as the buildings became lower it became much more difficult. Finally they were in an area that was all small houses similar to where they lived. Luckily Vince had only driven about three blocks when he parked. Titan was able to leap high and out of sight to stay with him and then land in a nearby alleyway. He quickly transformed and made his way to the mouth of the alley, peering carefully around the corner where he spotted Vince stepping away from the Olds.

Vince looked around carefully, and then began to walk. Michael came out of the alley after waiting a moment and followed. He did his best to keep a safe distance between himself and Vince. It was not easy in this deserted residential area. Michael often found himself ducking behind trees or bushes fearing that Vince may look back and spot him. He never did. Vince then turned another corner and arrived at St. Mary cemetery where he passed through the old gate.

Michael hadn't been to this place in far too long and was surprised that he never realized they were even near it. St. Mary's was a large gothic strip of land right at the edge of the east side of Delta City. It was one of the oldest cemeteries in the entire city, and full of mausoleums and big head stones, some even with massive statues. Michael felt more comfortable knowing now where they were headed. Even though the cemetery was practically empty, he found it easy to stay out of sight and follow Vince. When Vince stopped in front of a family plot headstone Michael didn't need to see the inscription, he knew it by heart already. It read, 'Here lies beloved parents Kathy and Kevin Novak'.

Michael crept through a tangle of head stones in a wide circle until he was once again facing Vince. He found a large grey stone that was resting beside a big maple tree and hid there. He watched as Vince stood solemnly and stared at the grave. Then he crumpled down to his knees with his head down. Michael froze afraid to move. He felt as though he were now encroaching on a private moment and was in the wrong.

Vince stood and Michael saw that his eyes were red and face streaked with tears. Michael couldn't even remember seeing Vince cry when they were younger. In fact Michael was hard pressed to remember a time when Vince had shown any sign of weakness around him.

After several minutes Vince turned and started walking back the way he had come. Michael stayed where he was for five minutes more then moved to where Vince had been standing, looking down at the resting place of his parents. It was then that he was struck by a deluge of memories of his older brother from when they were both much younger, and actually did get along. At that moment, Michael realized how right his grandfather had been. He wondered how things could possibly have gotten so bad between them. It had started long before Michael had found the ring. Perhaps, Michael thought, he had been too hard on Vince, and maybe he had largely misunderstood him.

CHAPTER 6: Hawk

"He was crying?" Carly exclaimed after Michael had recounted his story.

"Carly, you can't tell anyone. You may think I'm joking, but if Vince knew I was there following him I think he may really kill me," Michael responded.

After leaving the cemetery Michael had returned to the hospital to be with Grandpa Dale. He had spent the remainder of the day with him and did not leave until visiting hours had ended. He had not been able to reach Carly on her cell all day. Then, when he left the hospital his cell had died. He had meant to charge it once he got home, but was so tired he had flopped in bed and was asleep before he knew it. So, he wasn't able to talk to her until the next morning.

He had managed to blow off Dave and Perminder, which had been easy on a Saturday morning. Once his cell was charged, he made his way straight to her family's apartment. He was determined to avoid Carly's dad whenever possible so he had texted her on his way, and she had met him in the hall and they went right to the rooftop. Finally, he had been able to tell her everything from the day before.

It felt good to him to be able to confide in her once again. Since their near breakup which was now two days ago, he had found himself for the first time doubting the only thing in his life, besides his grandfather, that he had always assumed to be a certainty, and that was his close relationship with Carly. He felt renewed, even amidst all he was going through, just knowing they had reconnected made every challenge seem manageable. Things seemed awkward and surprisingly unfamiliar once they reconciled, but they quickly fell back into their old rhythms.

"What did Azure say about the whole thing?" Carly asked.

"I never had the chance to ask him. I had to transform quickly from Titan to keep up with Vince and never changed back to ask him," Michael said.

They were both leaning against the ledge looking over the street below, where not that long ago Michael had discovered the ring and this journey as Titan had begun. The sun was already up and blazing and it seemed it was going to be unseasonably hot again in Delta City.

"Well, what do you think was going on between him and Dylan?" Carly asked. "And don't worry, I won't say I told you so about Dylan either."

"Yeah, don't worry you don't have to. I already know it. I can only assume he was giving Vince money, but I have no clue what he was giving Dylan. I've gone over the whole thing so many times and I'm just so confused. Like, how did Vince get a car? Was it even his car?"

Carly put an arm over Michael's shoulders as he gazed over the city, and began to gently rub his back.

"Did you find out what started the fight between him and your grandpa at least?"

"No, but Grandpa Dale said it involved my parents. I want to ask him more, but I'm afraid it will upset him and he's still so weak. I don't dare try and get it out of Vince either," Michael said, dropping his head down in frustration.

"Plus, now I have this mad man using who knows what other kinds of weapons to attack the city, and I have no idea when he'll attack again either."

"Well, I think you need to talk to Vicki and see if she knows anything about this guy before something else major happens," Carly said.

"I know, I plan to today sometime. I just wish I could find out where he will strike next so I can be ready."

"Well, for now you better get going to your other job or you just might draw the wrath of Mr. Caruthers," Carly said, looking down at her watch.

Michael leaped to his feet and quickly planted a kiss on Carly's forehead and started for the door. Once there he turned back toward her.

"I'll call you as soon as my shift is over."

"You better," Carly said, with a wry smile, as she watched him vanish through the door.

Michael quickly jogged toward the store. He had completely lost track of time. He knew he could only push the goodwill of Mr. Caruthers so far before it reached its limits. He had decided to go in even though Mr. Caruthers wasn't expecting him. There wasn't much he could do for his grandpa besides sit around, and in the end the family needed the money. He didn't even dare to glance at his phone to check the time as he ran. He knew he would be cutting it close as it was.

Just as Michael was a block from the store he glanced to his right and all his plans suddenly changed. Above the lower east side apartments and buildings he saw three tall columns of smoke climbing into the sky. Michael's heart suddenly began to race as he screeched to a halt and stared at the smoke columns. He could practically feel the ring pulsating on his finger. He knew what job would have to take priority and dashed into the nearest alley to transform.

"Exaudio Fortis!"

Michael had become so accustomed to the transformation that he barely even changed the tempo of his strides. He simply let the lightning embrace him as he said the magic words. He relished the moment as the power coursed through his entire body. Suddenly, he felt invincible. His foot was searching for a hold to launch into the sky. In mere moments from first seeing the smoke rising Titan was soaring through the sky and bounding across rooftops towards the scene. He sliced through the air at ferocious speeds, the landscape below whizzing past while he assessed the exact location from where he was.

"We have trouble, Azure."

Is it another attack from our shadowy nemesis?

"Not sure yet, but I'm gonna go out on a limb and say that it is, from the signs of smoke up ahead."

Very well, we shall assess further once you arrive.

Titan found Azure's words puzzling, but he tried to ignore it. It had never occurred to him that there wasn't trouble. After all, if there was smoke was there not fire?

As Titan drew closer he saw that the smoke was coming from the Douglas Bridge on the edge of Delta City's downtown. The bridge was a Delta City landmark and one of the busiest routes into the city that crossed over the Sumac River. Two massive brick arches soared high above from either end of the bridge. As Titan came within a jump of the bridge he saw that there were several cars in flames and fires burning the bridge deck as well. One of the massive smoke columns that he had seen came from a tanker truck in flames. Suddenly, out of the corner of his eye he spotted a small craft flying around the bridge.

Just as Titan leaped to the top platform of the closest archway he saw that the small craft was not a craft at all but a man with a contraption strapped to his back. The contraption appeared to be a set of metal jet powered wings. Four jets were positioned at the top and bottom corners of the wings that allowed the man to fly. Strapped to the man's forearms were what seemed to be a set of weapons. He had a rocket launcher on one, and a machine gun on the other. Just as Titan's feet touched down on the top of the bridge, he saw a small rocket fire from the man's right arm, leaving a thin white trail of smoke hanging in the air. The rocket exploded in a ball of fire at the base of the bridge where a series of suspension cables were secured. The cables suddenly buckled leaving many to hang loose and dangle dangerously across the bridge deck.

"Well, it looks like it's our guy all right," Titan said to Azure.

Yes, it would appear so. As long as you can keep him as far from this bridge as possible you should have no problem detaining him. Remember, this is likely just another soldier of our true threat and we need to be able to question this man.

"I'll do what I can."

Titan poised himself for battle and watched as the flying man soared over the bridge and rocketed past the archway on which Titan stood. Titan raised his staff and fired a lightning blast at him. The blast narrowly missed a wing tip as he flew past. The man circled and re-directed himself toward Titan. Titan raised his staff once more preparing to fire again. However, the man suddenly pulled up and hovered just above Titan.

"You may have saved this city from my fellow soldier, Sonic, but I can guarantee you that you won't get so lucky with me. Now prepare to face Hawk!"

Without hesitation, Hawk raised both arms and fired at Titan. Titan began to run across the thirty feet of concrete platform of the arch with bullets racing around his feet. He turned in mid sprint with his staff raised while a rocket exploded at his side almost knocking him over the edge. Titan regained his footing and got off another lightning blast, colliding with the broad side of Hawk's left wing.

Hawk sputtered and dropped slightly as he grasped at what seemed to be a series of controls at his belt. Titan had no time to look; he leaped from the arch and caught one of the bridge's cables. While Titan clung to the cables, he could see Hawk struggle to regain full control of his wings. Titan tried to position himself with his staff ready to fire at Hawk again if needed. That's when he heard a maniacal laugh come from Hawk as he flew in front of Titan.

"If that's all you have then I truly am going to destroy your city, and you will be able to do nothing but watch, and then I'm going to destroy you!" Hawk bellowed as he hovered around Titan.

"We'll see about that," Titan said.

Titan wanted to say something more to Hawk but he was far too preoccupied with keeping himself perched high above the bridge deck. With a glance down he could see people scurry from their cars and scramble to safety at either end of the bridge. He could also see the flashing red and blue lights of the emergency responders at either end of the bridge. The emergency vehicles were not about to enter the bridge with the battle still raging. All civilians seemed in relative safety as they made their way on foot off the bridge.

Titan was focused on the public safety, but he also knew he had to be focused on the current danger at hand which was Hawk. He turned back, and saw Hawk bring his arms up, pointing them toward Titan. With little time to react Titan leaped forward, turned and fired a blast at Hawk. He could hear the hiss of machine gun fire as he plummeted downward.

Falling toward the bridge deck, Titan saw Hawk shift wildly, the blast barely missing him, Titan crashed onto the roof of an abandoned car. The car caved in, the edges of the roof closing in around him.

"You know, I think maybe I'll just destroy you first after all," Hawk declared. He angled himself down toward Titan, arms aimed and ready.

Bullets ricochet off the car with a series of pinging sounds. Titan, cautiously, climbed from the wreckage. He put up his arm to shield his face as bullets continued to fly past. He was able to see Hawk bearing down at him from the top of the bridge. He quickly turned to run and seek better shelter from the attack.

Titan you must seek shelter, and find a way to disable Hawk's weapons before he causes anyone harm.

"Yeah, tell me about it," Titan said. He dove and rolled under a big tanker truck.

Titan ducked behind one of the truck's tires. He could not tell where Hawk was. He looked up and all around but saw nothing. He could hear the fires burning and metal falling and crashing around the bridge, but that was no surprise with the damage the bridge had now sustained.

"You coward," Hawk bellowed. "You can't hide from me. I'll just tear down this whole bridge, and then you'll have no place left to hide."

Titan lowered his head at the sound of Hawk's voice, and peered from under the truck. He could see Hawk now standing on the bridge deck both arms bent at the elbow ready to strike as he searched for Titan. Pulling his staff into position, Titan aimed from under the truck to strike at Hawk. Before he could, however, he saw Hawk lower his right arm.

"I told you, you can't hide," Hawk said. He fired a rocket at the truck Titan was crouched under.

Titan tried to get to his feet as fast as he could, but even with super powered agility he simply wasn't fast enough. He hadn't taken more than one step when the rocket hit the truck and a warm wind engulfed him. Flames licked and grabbed at him. He was knocked face first into the trailer of a semi-truck. Titan felt his body go slack as he peeled himself off the massive dent in the trailer and fell to the road in a heap. The heat of the fire was so intense that Titan was forced to look away, and was unable to see

Hawk anywhere.

Titan, are you alright?

"I'm not too sure how to answer that right now," Titan said, as he slowly staggered to his feet.

His costume was now in tatters. He bled from the many cuts and scrapes that now littered his body. His nose bled profusely. He felt like a tender peach, fresh bruises popped up all over his battered body. He knew that his powers would have these wounds healed before he could even transform back to himself, but that didn't dull the pain he felt at that moment.

"Where are you?" Hawk bellowed, from the other side of the burning truck.

"Okay, time to put an end to this guy," Titan, said under his breath.

Yes, the people are safe, but we should take this opportunity to extract information about his shadowy master.

Titan could hear bursts of machine gun fire and the clattering of brick, metal, and glass. He had no idea if Hawk was trying to flush him out or simply trying to lay waste to the bridge. Titan peaked around the truck and saw police cruisers at the far end of the bridge, but none were attempting to cross and engage with Hawk.

"Okay, I'm gonna get this loser and make him talk," Titan said. He shifted, coiling himself into a tight ball ready to spring out at any moment.

Titan sprang into action launching himself over the truck, staff in hand and ready to fire. Hawk was facing the side of the bridge hovering a few feet in the air spraying bullets over the dozens of deserted cars. Hawk turned his head toward Titan and began to aim his arm cannons his way but did not get very far. A big bolt of blue lightning leaped from the tip of Titan's staff and connected with the joint of his left wing. Hawk, who was flying slowly down the expanse of the bridge suddenly locked up and crashed down to the surface and skidded to a stop on the asphalt.

Titan pounced on Hawk as he lay in a crumpled heap. He pinned one arm with his leg and grabbed hold of the other with his right hand firmly. Hawk's struggles to free himself were in vain.

"This will end right now! You are going to tell me where I can find your boss and anything else this lunatic may have planned for the city," Titan said, moving mere inches from Hawk's face.

"You think you scare me? The Doc will destroy you!" Hawk screeched. He writhed around in vain, attempting to break free of Titan's grasp.

"What do you mean? What does he have planned?" Titan asked again.

"You're pathetic. All you can do is detain me briefly until he comes for me, and he will come. This city will be the first to fall to him."

"What am I supposed to do here? I'm sorta new at the whole interrogation game," Titan asked Azure in a low voice as he tilted his head away from Hawk slightly.

This man appears unstable. I am unsure what use he will be to us in the end.

"So what am I supposed to do then?" Titan asked.

Hawk took the opportunity to try and push Titan off and get free. Titan held strong. He picked Hawk up, and shoved him against the rail of the bridge.

"You move again and I'll tear off your little wings and throw you over the side!" Titan declared.

We should drop him to the authorities. They can get the answers from him. It may also earn you some much needed credibility with this city's law enforcement.

"Now you're talking my language," Titan replied.

Before he had a chance to react, however, he could hear the whoop, whoop sounds of a helicopter not far off. Titan scanned all around the horizon and saw nothing. Then, rising into view from below the bridge was a full sized military helicopter. Staring through the glass at Titan was the same military commander from the tank. Its guns seemed aimed directly at Titan. He could see the commander raise a mike to his face.

"Hold it right there or we will fire!" bellowed the commander over the loudspeaker.

CHAPTER 7: Aerial Attack

"I repeat, stand down now!" the army commander demanded again over the loudspeaker.

"I think he's talking to you," Hawk hissed.

Titan still had Hawk by the forearms and pinned against the bridge rail. Titan looked all around him checking his complete surroundings. There was only this one helicopter hovering just over them. The authorities still remained at either end of the bridge in order to hold Titan and Hawk from escaping the bridge that way.

"Don't think you'll get a…"

Before Titan could finish, as he was still slightly distracted from Hawk, a small mechanical arm popped out of the back of Hawk's wings and rested high above his shoulders. Three mini rockets fried from the arm right at Titan's head and chest the moment it was in place. Titan finally let go of Hawk to deflect the rockets from his face. The rockets were small but stung as they exploded off Titan's arms. It was all the distraction that Hawk needed, however.

Once Titan let go, Hawk blasted into the air. Hawk turned and fired at the army helicopter. The helicopter had to switch to evasive maneuvers to avoid the attack. With both the helicopter and Titan momentarily diverted, Hawk had all the time he needed to make an escape. Titan regained full composure and moved to attack and defend, but Hawk had already risen high above the bridge and turned back toward the city.

Titan, this will escalate quickly if Hawk reaches the city. Many lives could be at risk and much of the city could be destroyed. We do not know yet just how much fire power he is capable of.

"I'm on it, Azure. It could be tricky though with these army guys around," Titan said, as he leaped to the bridge's highest point.

59

As if on cue the helicopter dropped and flew low over the water as it approached the city right on Hawk's trail. The helicopter reached the skyline and rose high into the air so it could look down over the city's downtown skyscrapers. Hawk had soared over the authorities at the end of the bridge and vanished into the dense city sprawl.

"Okay, great, looks like I have some catching up to do," Titan said.

Titan coiled his legs and launched himself at the city. Typically, he would leap up and over to wherever he needed to go. Now he needed to stay fairly low so he could stay on Hawk's trail. He soared over the scrambling police and emergency workers who were now attempting to leave their posts and follow the impending action. Titan landed on the flag pole of a building at the edge of the city. He could see Hawk several blocks up rocketing just over head of the grid locked traffic. Titan leaped forward to a building ledge that should have put him almost right on top of Hawk.

Titan, you cannot keep up with Hawk at this rate. You must get ahead of him if you ever intend to apprehend him.

"I'll do what I can, he's not exactly holding still for me though," Titan replied, while he got a foot hold for his landing.

As soon as he landed Hawk sped past him. Titan watched Hawk look over his shoulder and took notice of him. He was looking to leap forward and get him when he saw Hawk fire a series of rockets toward the city below him. Explosions rang out as Titan watched fire and dust and debris fly into the air. Titan quickly pulled himself back and clung to the ledge of the building.

"What do we do here, Azure? These people will need help, but if I stay here, Hawk may get away." Titan asked.

He is using the people against you. He knows your main objective is their safety. He must preoccupy you to get away. Scan the area for any emergency and then resume your pursuit. Let others clean up this mess, we must catch Hawk.

"Okay, you're the boss," Titan said, as he dropped to street level.

People were screaming and running frantically. Nothing at first seemed in immediate danger. Then Titan heard a piercing scream that cut through the clatter and commotion. One of Hawk's rockets had hit a third floor balcony that faced the street. The balcony was severely damaged and hung from the side of the building by a lone steel bracket. On it, a young blonde woman clung for dear life. She hung over the sidewalk three stories below.

Titan easily leaped to the ledge next to the dilapidated balcony. The young woman had her fingers tightly wrapped around one iron rail, but they were slipping every second.

"Hold on, I'll get you!" Titan yelled out to her.

Titan dropped to the ledge one floor down. He quickly repositioned his feet. He noticed a large crowd start to gather below. The young woman screamed again as the bracket began to give way and the balcony dropped down causing her grip to loosen.

"Okay, when I say, I want you to let go," Titan instructed.

"Are you crazy?" she squealed.

"Just trust me."

Titan gave the young woman a moment to get ready. He knew she would not have much more than that however. He reached his one arm out as far as he could, preparing himself for her fall.

"Okay, now!"

Despite her fears the young blonde did not hesitate. She released what was left of her grip. Titan wrapped his extended arm around her waist as he pushed off the side of the building. The two seemed to be suspended in midair like a couple of cartoon characters for the briefest of moments. Titan already had a firm grip when she wrapped her arms tightly around his neck. Titan managed to drop to street level as gently as he could.

Once they landed in the street, the crowd broke into loud cheers. Titan could feel the young blonde's knees buckle as he started to let her go. If she had not been clinging tightly to him she would have hit the ground. Titan helped her back to her feet. He turned to leave and resume his chase of Hawk when he felt the girl grab his arm and pull him back toward her. Before he knew what was happening she planted a kiss firmly on his mouth. At that, the crowd only cheered louder. Several people began to move in with camera phones pointed at the pair.

"Thanks," she said softly, pulling away from Titan.

"Um, no problem," Titan replied. He quickly turned away and leaped back to the rooftops. "Man, I will be in so much trouble for that," He whispered to himself

Titan began to resume his chase where he left off. He could now hear approaching police sirens coming from all angles. Occasionally, as he soared past he saw the flashing red and blue lights of cruisers in pursuit. He was leaping across the city watching for any signs of Hawk having passed through when he suddenly saw him fly right past him, heading to his right. Titan quickly tried to change course and follow. As he began to turn, he found himself right in the path of the military helicopter. It was directly behind him and moving fast following Hawk. The wind kicked up by the helicopter blades was so intense that Titan could practically feel the blades pass directly above his head, narrowly missing him.

Titan had to quickly angle himself away from the helicopter before it passed right through him. Having lost complete control, he flew at the buildings along the street and crashed into a massive gothic style apartment building. He shot through part of the wall and window and crashed into the adjoining apartment. Glass and brick crashed in all around him with some debris falling to the street below. Titan quickly gathered his bruised and beaten body and went back to the giant hole in the wall he had come through. He glanced back over his shoulder and glimpsed a young boy sitting cross legged and playing with a couple of toy trucks.

"Whoa, are you okay?" the little boy asked, eyes wide as he stared at Titan and pointed at a series of cuts on Titan's left arm.

"Yeah, I think I'll live," Titan replied, as he climbed to the edge of the hole in the wall.

"Are you sure? 'Cause I can get my Mom. She has all kinds of band aids she can give you."

"Thanks, little man, but I really have to get going. I have a bad guy I need to stop." Titan braced himself by grabbing both edges of the crumbling wall and peering out into the street looking either way. "Be good, okay, pal."

"Okay, I will," the little boy whispered as Titan leaped from the opening.

Titan landed on the top of the adjacent building and began scanning for Hawk. He was sprinting across the roof listening and looking all over for landmarks to guide himself by. Then, ahead to his right, Titan spotted a cloud of dust rise into the air and heard the rumble of falling brick and mortar that followed, as well as the screaming crowd caught in the attack. Then he saw the helicopter circling around a set of skyscrapers and angled down at the source of the attack.

"Okay, here goes nothing," Titan said, leaping into the air and into the fray.

You must get to Hawk and disable him once and for all. You can worry about the helicopter afterwards. It is only a matter of time before there are serious civilian injuries.

"Yeah, I'm pretty sick of this guy already, so I fully plan to end this right now," Titan replied, jumping over the ledge and dropped to the street.

Titan saw the street below plunged into utter chaos. It was littered with big chunks of cinder blocks, metal, and glass. Several cars had been crushed in the explosion and resulting rain of debris. Two of the buildings facing the intersection had big gaping holes spewing fire that appeared to be Hawk's handy work. Titan's body hung above the street before making contact and landing against a building facing the street. He saw the helicopter swing in low just below him and move to the side. It kicked up big gusts of air as Titan clung and positioned himself against the building.

Then, he saw Hawk rocket out from between two other buildings firing machine gun blasts all over the streets below.

Titan perched himself precariously to a window ledge seemingly unnoticed by both Hawk and the helicopter crew. Both seemed locked in an air duel of which only the people of Delta City seemed destined to lose. Both flew just below Titan. He could only afford to wait a short time before jumping into the fray himself. Finally he got his opening as Hawk swung wide around the open square looking to avoid the helicopter's wrath and reposition himself to attack it. Hawk came one floor below him and fifteen yards away from the face of the building when Titan made his move.

Titan leaped from the window ledge and landed squarely on Hawk's back. He gripped both of his wings tightly with each hand. Hawk let out a loud yelp and dropped twenty feet with the sudden added weight of Titan on his back. Titan watched closely as the helicopter swung around to face them. It positioned its belly guns directly at the two of them. Titan knew he only had seconds to act. If he hesitated, the helicopter would not. Hawk started to spin wildly around the cluster of buildings trying desperately to regain control of his wings. The helicopter had to pull back to avoid colliding with them.

"I will not let you do any more damage!" Titan yelled, still gripping the wings firmly. He took his right hand off the wing to make his move.

"Oh, we'll just see about that," Hawk replied.

With a simple flick of his finger Hawk began to rocket straight up into the air. Titan had no choice but to quickly grab on with his right hand and hold on. Within seconds Hawk had soared into the air, the entire city now resting below them. Struggling with his grip, Titan pulled down hard with his left hand to try and bring Hawk down. Titan saw the city pass by him as they twirled and spun across the city skyline. Before they could regain control, Titan noticed that they had passed back over the harbor. He quickly saw his opening and took it. With one quick punch he rammed his fist through Hawk's right wing.

Titan finally let go, plunging sharply to the harbor below. Just as he splashed down, he saw Hawk crash into the water about thirty feet away with a mighty splash. Underwater and swimming back up toward the light of the surface, Titan could see the silhouette of the military helicopter swoop overhead. Titan surfaced and swam in place, watching intently as the helicopter hovered over the spot where Hawk went in.

Titan started to make his way to shore, fifty yards away, and kept checking back over his shoulder to see if Hawk would pop up. By the time Titan crawled out of the water onto wet mud, Hawk had still not resurfaced.

"I don't know what's going on. I find it very hard to believe that Hawk died from that fall," Titan said to Azure.

It does seem unlikely. I am afraid that we may have to wait and face him another time. If he does surface he should be incapacitated and able to be apprehended by the military authorities.

"Okay, sounds good, we should get out..." Titan began before being cut off.

"Don't move, remain right where you are!" shouted a commanding voice from up on the bank behind him.

Without thinking, Titan whirled around and found himself face to face with a man he had seen numerous times in the Courier and on TV, Chief Ross. Behind Chief Ross stood another plainclothes detective Titan had seen before, and about a half dozen other uniformed police officers. All of the officers except Chief Ross had their guns drawn and aimed right at him. Titan instinctively took one step back.

"I know you have a lot of superpowers, but maybe hearing isn't one of them. I said not to move," Chief Ross said.

"Well, that may be a problem," Titan said. "Because I'm afraid I can't let you take me."

"I'm afraid that's not up to you," Ross replied.

Chief Ross never lost his composure or tone of authority as he stood before Titan. He had one arm extended back to his officers to hold them back from taking a shot, the other arm extended toward Titan so there could be no mistaking who he was commanding to step down. The other officers all seemed to have wide eyed nervous looks on their faces, and a couple were clutching revolvers with shaky hands.

"Believe it or not, I am on your side, you know," Titan said, very conscious not to move at all.

"If you were on our side you would have one of those uniforms on," Chief Ross said, nodding his head back to the officers behind him.

Just then, out in the harbor to their left, the helicopter fired two rockets into the water where Hawk had gone down. A funnel of water about twenty feet high shot into the air as the rockets hit. Titan was the only one on shore who did not bother to look. While Chief Ross and his men looked out over the harbor at the commotion, Titan leapt up into the air with all his might. The mud had made it difficult to push off with as much force as he would have liked, but he still got high enough into the air to be out of range of the officers. He came down into downtown and barrel rolled onto a skyscraper rooftop. Once there, he looked back over the harbor and could still see the helicopter panning around the shoreline in search of Hawk. He could no longer see the police or hear any sirens, but could assume he had lost them for good.

"Well, that was close," Titan said once he could lean up against the duct on the rooftop.

That was very lucky. We will have to come up with a strategy to handle the authorities here.

"Yeah, I agree. I can't keep dodging them like this. Did all the other Titans have this problem?"

No, but these are very different times.

"Oh man, I have to get going. Mr. Caruthers is going to be so mad that I'm this late," Titan said.

Very well, there is little else that can be done about Hawk. You disabled him from destroying any more of the city. We will discuss the rest in greater detail later.

With that Titan began to bound his way across the city and to the alley behind Caruthers Grocery. He dropped into the alley behind the store and prepared to transform hastily.

"Extermino Fortis!"

Before Michael could even turn around and head for the store entrance facing the alley, he heard a familiar voice, but in a range he had never heard before.

"Mike! No way!" Perminder's voice came from behind him.

Michael spun around on his heels, and found himself face to face with Perminder. A fountain soda cup fell to the ground, its dark liquid contents spilling around his feet.

"You're Titan!" Perminder practically screamed. "Have you been Titan this whole time?"

"Perminder, I swear this isn't how it looks."

"Really, then how does it look?"

Michael only stood there with his mouth hung open and lips moving, and no words coming out and smoke dissipated around him.

"Yeah, exactly," he said, referring to Michael's speechlessness. "How could you not tell me about this, man?"

"Novak, what are you doing out here? You were supposed to be at work over an hour ago. This is the thanks I get for helping you out while your grandfather is sick?" Mr. Caruthers' voice boomed as he flung open the back door of the store.

"Um...I'm sorry, Mr. Caruthers," Michael said, turning from Perminder to his boss and back again.

"Not half as sorry as you'll be if you don't get in here right away, and starts working on pricing all those canned beans you were supposed to have done an hour ago," Mr. Caruthers hollered, turning and heading back into the store.

Michael took a step toward the door and then hesitated. He was glad to have been interrupted by Mr. Caruthers since he had no idea how to handle Perminder having seen him as Titan. He also knew, however, that he could not just leave Perminder with that piece of information and just hope he could keep a lid on it.

"Oh man, who else knows about this?" Perminder asked, his eyes still wide in disbelief. Michael wasn't even sure if he had seen Perminder blink once since seeing him.

"Just Carly, and now you. Look, you can't say a word about this to anyone. You have no idea how important that is."

"I can tell Dave though, right?"

"No one! I mean it," Michael said raising a finger at Perminder's face to drive the point home.

"NOVAK!" Mr. Caruthers bellowed from the store.

"Look I have to go before Mr. Caruthers blows a gasket," Michael said moving to the door. He opened it and turned back before stepping inside. "I'll meet you at Carly's right after work, okay? I'll fill you in on everything then. Just don't say anything to absolutely anyone until that time. Can you do that?"

"Hey, I'm not sure that anybody would believe me anyway," Perminder said, breaking into a broad smile. "I can't believe it, you're Titan. You, Michael Novak, are really Titan."

"Yes, now remember, not a word to anyone. I'll see you just after five at Carly's."

Michael stepped inside and closed the door behind him. The door clicked shut and the last thing Michael saw was Perminder, still staring at him wide eyed and smiling like some kid all excited about his birthday presents. Michael then threw on his smock, grabbed his pricing gun off the shelf and took a box of the canned beans into the store.

It had taken some time, but Michael had eventually managed to find a way to wrap his head around how his life could go from battling a villain such as Hawk across the entire city to being at Caruthers' Grocery stocking shelves within twenty minutes. His life was constantly teeter-tottering from the normal and mundane to the surreal.

He could hear Mr. Caruthers puttering around at the front of the store and wasn't sure if he should try and apologize or just avoid him for the rest of the day. Avoiding his boss had become one of his specialties of the past months, but he also didn't like the idea that Mr. Caruthers was thinking that he was taking advantage of his grandfather being ill. Michael made his way down the aisle and turned toward the front counter of the store where Mr. Caruthers sat perched in his usual spot on his stool at the cash register. Thankfully, Michael thought, there were no customers present in the store.

"Uh, Mr. Caruthers, I just wanted to say that I'm real sorry that I was late, and that I really do have a good excuse," Michael said, stepping up to the counter.

"A good excuse, eh? You call hangin' around with one of your buddies out back a good excuse. Just what were you doing back there for over an hour anyway?"

"No, that wasn't it I swear. I just bumped into Perminder coming into the back of the store."

"Well, we'll just see the next time I do you any more favors. Now, I do believe you have some more stocking and pricing to do."

Michael turned away and went back into the stock room. His grandpa had always told him that actions speak louder than words. Next time he would just have to listen to his gut and forget the talking and simply avoid the wrath of Mr. Caruthers. For the rest of his shift he did just that, while counting down the minutes until he could get to Carly's where hopefully Perminder would be there waiting and, with luck, he had been able to keep his mouth shut about Titan.

CHAPTER 8: City Under Siege

"This is so crazy! You, Michael Novak, are Titan. How could you not have told me this before? I can't believe I found out this way. I can't believe I am just finding this out!" Perminder said, pacing around the rooftop waving his arms about animatedly.

"I'm sorry you had to find out that way, but I just couldn't tell you. You have to understand that," Michael said, sitting at the old bus bench that made up some of their helter-skelter furniture collection on the rooftop.

Michael had gotten through the rest of his shift at Caruthers' Grocery with no more negative encounters with Mr. Caruthers. Yet, he knew his lateness was far from forgotten by the old shop keeper. Once he had finished, he had rushed to Carly's finding a very anxious Perminder and a quite annoyed Carly waiting for him. Carly had instantly given him a look which Michael interpreted as her saying 'how could you tell him.' He knew he would have to explain to her later.

"I really am sorry I had to lie to you about this," Michael repeated, hoping at least for a change of expression.

"You should be sorry, keeping something this big from me. Dude, I thought we were best buds. I never take the shortcut through the alley. If it wasn't for that I still wouldn't have a clue," Perminder continued.

"Well, it's not like you're known as the best secret keeper," Carly said, sitting on an old patio chair by the table.

"Carly, I'm hurt. I would never betray Mike like that," Perminder said.

"She didn't mean it that way, right?" Michael said, trying to defuse the situation. He looked at Carly who only rolled her eyes and turned her head away from them both.

"So, what's the deal? Come on, tell me the whole story of how this happened," Perminder asked.

Perminder took a seat at one of the other patio chairs opposite Carly and listened intently as Michael told him his story of Titan. For nearly an hour Perminder sat in rapt attention while Michael told him about how he got the ring, about Azure, his battle with Mr. Midnight's organization and the motion inhibitor, and his current struggles. He had never even seen Perminder pay half as close attention in any of his classes before. He glanced over several times at Carly while he told his story and saw her nervously biting her lower lip and wringing her fingers together. He knew she was uneasy about Perminder knowing his secret, but he could see no other choice, especially considering how he found out.

"Wow, man. No wonder you've been acting so weird lately," Perminder said, once Michael had finished.

"Azure forbids me from telling anyone. I was only able to have Carly in on it because she was there when I found the ring. It would have been kind of hard to keep her out of the loop," Michael said.

"Perminder," Carly said, reaching across the table and resting her hand on his arm to ensure his full attention. "I hope you realize how important this is. You can't tell a soul about any of this."

Perminder's eyes narrowed and he leaned back into his chair letting out a big sigh.

"You know, you guys aren't showing a lot of faith in me here. I do get this you know. I would never put Mike, or any of us, in jeopardy by saying anything. I won't even tell Dave, okay?" Perminder said, throwing up his hands in clear frustration in their lack of trust in his secret keeping abilities. "Dave doesn't know does he? Please tell me you didn't tell him and not me."

"No he doesn't know, and he definitely can't know right now. I just can't help but feel uneasy when I see him hanging around my brother," Michael said. "I know my brother has been involved in criminal activity. I was only able to use Titan to scare him so much before he went back to it. I can't risk Vince finding out about any of this."

"Wow, this whole thing has made you have some serious trust issues," Perminder said.

"We're not saying we don't trust you. It's just no one else has found out yet, so you know, this is kind of a big deal. Trust us here, this is no easy secret to keep," Michael said, trying to reassure Perminder as best he could.

"So, when I saw you today, I take it you had just come from that whole dust up down at the bridge?" Perminder asked.

"Yes. This new mystery guy is proving to be more of a pain than Mr. Midnight. He's causing some serious problems right now," Michael responded.

"I saw on TV that the military showed up again," Carly added.

"Yeah, at first I thought they were here for me. I think they're actually tracking down the boss of Sonic and Hawk," Michael said.

"Why would they bring in the military for some bad guy terrorizing our city? The police didn't even get a chance to handle it on their own," Perminder asked.

"I don't know. I don't even really know what I'm facing at all, yet. The whole situation keeps evolving all the time," Michael said.

"The mayor was sure trying to imply that they were here for you," Carly said.

"No, they had their chance; both times, to take me out, or at least try,"

"Try, eh? Listen to you now. I think if the military wanted they could make a pretty good try even for Titan," Perminder said, with a grin.

"Well, my point is they didn't try," Michael said, with a slight roll of his eyes.

"Yeah, and speaking of your little performance today, we can talk later about that woman you kissed in the street," Carly said, with a raise of the eyebrow.

"Ooh, busted, man" Perminder said, barely able to hold in his laughter.

Michal blushed and hung his head.

The three of them sat and talked for some time after that until Perminder finally stood and said he had to leave. Michael and Perminder had agreed to meet up alone and walk to school together. Carly and Michael walked to the doorway with Perminder, and said their goodbyes. When the door was finally shut, Michael hadn't felt more relieved in ages to have been able to tell one of his best friends about his biggest secret.

"You think he can really manage to keep his mouth shut about all this?" Carly asked once Perminder was gone.

"I actually think he can," Michael said, trying to sound confident.

Carly turned and wrapped her arms around his neck, something she had not done since they had had their big fight.

"You know, Michael, I think the real issue here is that you are becoming addicted to being Titan," Carly declared.

"What are you talking about?" Michael replied.

"Well, let's see, you left me to take your grandfather to the hospital, you fled at the first sign of smoke today, and you dropped behind Caruthers' store when you were still Titan and let Perminder see you. I think you look for the first sign of needing to turn to Titan and then take it. You also wait as long as possible before turning back, like when Grandpa Dale had his heart attack," Carly said.

Michael said nothing in response. He hadn't even considered this before. He closed his eyes and envisioned the lightning taking him and transforming him into Titan. He felt the power flow through him. There was no denying the allure of the power. When he was Titan he felt invincible. All his real problems just melted away.

"You need to give a little more attention to everything else before you just fly off," Carly said.

"Okay, I promise, I'll do my very best," Michael replied.

There was a pause as they both looked at each other. Michael put out his hand, and Carly reached out and took it. He pulled her in close, wrapping his arms around her waist.

"Now, about this woman," she said, with a coy smile.

"Carly, I swear I did nothing to encourage that. I didn't even see it coming."

"It's okay, don't worry," Carly replied. Michael's face scrunched together in confusion, and Carly burst right out laughing. "I've thought about it, and I have come to realize that there are just certain things that I have to get accustomed to if I am going to be dating a superhero. If one of those is going to be your rabid female fan base, then so be it," Carly said, grinning broadly.

"Are you sure you're not just saying you're not mad but secretly you are and at some point this is going to come back and bite me?" Michael asked.

Carly's mouth dropped open in surprise as she pulled away and gave Michael a light smack on the arm.

"Michael, how dare you even think I would act that way."

"Okay, I'm sorry. I didn't mean anything by it," Michael said, reaching out and trying to take her hand, and pull her in close.

"It just so happens," said Carly. "That I've done a lot of thinking, you know, about us. I know I need to try and be more understanding about what you have to go through. I just never thought that I would have to go through this kind of drama in life, let alone while I was going through high school. Although, I think it may actually be easier now that Perminder knows too. At least I'll have someone who can kind of relate to what's going on."

"Good, then I'm glad he found out after all." Michael glanced at his watch. "Oh man, I better get going. I still have to call Grandpa Dale at the hospital and finish up some homework."

Michael gave Carly a quick kiss and headed for the door himself. He let his fingers slide over her hand and then stepped into the doorway and turned away.

"Oh, and Michael," Carly called to him. Michael turned back to her in mid stride. "Please be careful when transforming to and from Titan from now on. Maybe just have a quick look around first."

"I'll have to try that," Michael replied with a smile.

Michael bounded down the stairs of Carly's building two at a time and hit the sidewalk feeling surprisingly good considering that his day had not gotten off to a great start. Yet, having Perminder, one of his best friends, finally know about Titan lifted a huge weight off his shoulders.

Michael was about to round the corner for home, when he glanced further down the street and saw Dave come out of the Burger Shack. He was about to go over and say hi when he saw Vince come out right after him. The two had clearly been inside together and seemed in mid-conversation as Michael observed them exiting. Michael found himself frozen in place. The only thing that got him moving was the idea one of them would notice him standing there gawking at them. He quickly stepped behind the big lamppost by the curb.

He continued watching as they finished talking. Then, they shook hands and he watched Vince climb back into the old car he had been using the other day, leaving Dave standing on the sidewalk. Michael quickly turned and headed for home using an alternate route. The last thing he wanted, after seeing that, was to talk to either of them. He knew it shouldn't bother him seeing one of his closest friends talking to his brother, but knowing what he did about Vince it couldn't help but upset him.

When Michael finally got home the house was empty. It was exactly as Michael had left it. It didn't look as though Vince had been home since Michael had left that morning. He grabbed his school books, went in and plopped down on the living room sofa. He glanced over at the empty recliner and felt a pang of guilt. He had not gone to visit Grandpa Dale in the hospital. Michael reached over to the end table, picked up the phone and dialed. He hit the extension to his grandfather's room and waited.

"Hello," Grandpa Dale said, sounding sleepy.

"Hi, Grandpa, it's Michael. I hope I didn't wake you."

"Oh, it's okay. You know how it is, nothing to do here but sleep so I was just having a little cat nap."

"How're you feeling?" Michael asked.

"Me? I have no complaints. Just a little anxious to get home that's all," Grandpa Dale said.

"Well, I'm sorry I didn't get down to see you today. I had work and now I'm swamped with homework, but I swear I'll be down tomorrow," Michael promised.

"Oh, don't worry so much about me. I know you're busy. The doctor did say that I should be able to go home in a day or two anyhow," Grandpa Dale said.

"That's great, Grandpa. "

The two spoke for a few more minutes and then Michael hung up intending to start on some homework. Before he knew it, however, he had the TV on watching news recaps of his battle with Hawk. According to the reports, there was still no sign of Hawk. The footage showed all of the battle on the bridge and of course Hawk's crash landing in the water. The arrival of the military helicopter was spoken of, but very little footage shown. In press conferences shortly after the incident the mayor and Chief Ross would not indicate whether the military was there to intercept Titan or Hawk. Naturally the mayor tried his best to make it sound as though it was

Titan they were after.

Nothing new was said about the shadowy figure who seemed to be the puppet master of these events. Unlike last time, there were no threatening public announcements made. Though, Michael knew this attack came from the same shadowy figure. Chief Ross said very little and was evasive when asked about how close they came to apprehending Titan. The encounter had apparently been captured by an eyewitness camera phone that showed some shaky images of Titan being cornered by the police at the water's edge.

Michal had finally had enough. He set his school books aside, got up and got ready for bed. He tossed and turned for hours in the dark with so many thoughts swirling through his mind. So much had happened over the last week, he wasn't sure how much more he could take.

At some point, however, he must have drifted off to sleep, because, the next thing he knew he was being woken by loud knocking at the door. Rays of sunshine were blinding as he crawled out of bed and headed for the door.

"Man, tell me you've been watching the news," Perminder said, when Michael opened the door. He was panting heavily and very jumpy and excited.

"News? What news?" Michael asked, still trying to shake away the last vestiges of sleep.

"How could you not be in on this stuff, man. You're Titan for crying out loud," Perminder said, moving through the house and went straight to the TV.

"Uh, I thought we talked about discretion. You know Vince lives here too, right?"

"Don't worry he's not here. I saw him walking somewhere on my way here, and don't worry I steered way clear of him."

Michael came over to the TV which was once again showing a news conference. This time it was just Chief Ross at the podium with a military man in the background. It was the same man Michael had seen in both the tank and the helicopter.

Chief Ross was in the middle of discussing some attacks the night before. One was at a night club while the other was at a theater. In both cases it seemed that the floor had opened up and dozens of small robots had come out attacking the people there. There had been no fatalities, but many wounded. Some were wounded by the robots and others in the stampede of people that had ensued at both locations. There had been a message from the same shadowy figure once again claiming responsibility for the attacks.

"Oh man, this is not good," Michael said, staring dumbstruck at the TV. They were now showing some of the aftermath of the nightclub incident. It looked as though a wrecking ball had torn through the location and done some serious damage.

"I thought you got like some kind of warning or something when these things were going down," Perminder said.

"Afraid it doesn't work that way, but right now I wish it did."

"So, what are you going to do about all this?" asked Perminder.

"I have no idea," Michael responded.

"You're Titan! Aren't you supposed to go kick someone's butt?" said Perminder excitedly.

"Yeah, but whose?" Michael responded.

The screen then flashed back to Chief Ross.

"In light of these recent events and the threat the city remains under, I am afraid that we will be putting Delta City under curfew and enacting travel restrictions throughout the city. Any events or large public gatherings will be cancelled until further notice. If the attacks continue to escalate we will be at full blown martial law until such a time that the streets of our city can once again be deemed safe," said Chief Ross, looking gravely into the camera.

"You gotta do something, man," Perminder whispered, while they both stared into the TV as more images of the attacks flashed across the screen.

"I'll keep doing my best, but this guy has to poke his head out first," said Michael.

"What does all these new rules even mean anyway? It sounds more like something out of a movie," Perminder said, looking confused.

"I think we're about to find out," Michael said, as he heard his phone vibrate on the kitchen table.

Michael got up, went to the table, picked up his phone and flipped it open. It was a text from Carly asking if he had heard any of the news about the attacks. Michael answered and went back to the TV where Perminder still sat, eyes glued to the screen.

"Come on, we better get going," Michael said.

They left the house and began to make their way to school. Along the way Perminder continued to ask questions about Titan and all the powers Michael had when he was in costume. It went much as Michael thought it would, with Perminder's awe and fascination coming out. It was the main reason he wanted a chance to talk with him alone. He answered all the questions, and was actually grateful to be able to finally talk about it with him. Michael considered wearily whether they should pass by Dave's or not. He didn't want to alert Perminder to any of his suspicions yet, so they went by. Dave was nowhere to be seen, however, a few blocks later the two of them met Carly and Monica a block from the school.

"Good morning, ladies," Perminder exclaimed, and gave them a deep bow.

"You're such a loser," Monica grumbled. She turned and continued along her way.

"Where's Dave this morning?" Carly asked.

"Don't know, he wasn't around when we went by his place," Michael responded.

"Is that why you're acting weirder than usual, Perminder? I always knew you guys couldn't operate individually," Monica said, full of sarcasm.

"Uh… me no understand," Perminder said while crossing his eyes and staring aimlessly at the sky.

The four of them continued and were at the school five minutes later. When they got to school there was much more than the usual bustle of activity. It looked to Michael as though the entire faculty was out at various points of the school property directing the students about. There were also a lot of extra vehicles around. Several white panel vans and big dark blue sedans were parked on the street in front of the school. The principal, Mrs. Gervis, was standing at the top of the stairs at the school's main entrance with a megaphone.

"All students are to report to the school auditorium immediately for a special assembly," her voice bellowed through the megaphone.

"Well, you're right, buddy, looks like we are going to find out all about the state of things pretty quickly," Perminder said to Michael, as they made their way up the main path to the front steps of the school and right past Mrs. Gervis.

"I knew I should have stayed home today," Monica said, as they went inside.

They made their way into the main auditorium and took some seats in the top corner of the bleachers waiting for the other students to file in. At last the entire faculty entered and stood along the back of the auditorium floor. Mrs. Gervis was the last to enter, along with a man in a suit Michael had never seen before. The whole scene gave Michael a sense of increased uneasiness. Mrs. Gervis wasted no time, as soon as the clock on the back wall read eight thirty; she approached the podium that was set up in the center of the gym.

"Good day, students," she began. "As you have most likely heard already, there have been some rather serious attacks against our city over that last several days. In light of these recent and continued threats, the city is under increased security."

Mrs. Gervis paused here looking around the auditorium to ensure she had the students' full attention.

"What these extra security measures mean for us is that school will run largely as it always has, but with some minor adjustments. School starts promptly at eight thirty. Once the final bell rings the school will be closed and locked up. No one will enter or leave other than for emergencies until final bell at quarter past three. That means no going outdoors without approval until that time. When you do leave, you are to go directly home. There is now a mandatory curfew for all minors, which in effect means that anyone outdoors after sunset for unauthorized or unnecessary activity will be taken in by police for questioning." At this there was some grumbling and murmuring from the students.

"It is important that we remember students, that these measures are being taken for your own wellbeing. Now, I also want to introduce someone special today. Mr. Anderson please step forward." The man in the suit stepped up front beside Mrs. Gervis. "Mr. Anderson, who is with the superintendent's office, will be overseeing a small group of extra security that will be monitoring our school as well. This is being done for all major public places such as schools, hospitals, and shopping centres during these times."

At this Michael felt his stomach drop to the floor. He had just assumed that his grandpa would be safe because he was at the hospital, but hearing that there was going to be added security there made him feel uneasy.

"There is really nothing more to say at this time as we are all learning how to do this as we go, so please bear with us. Now, please go to your regularly scheduled class, and if your class is supposed to be outside or leaving the school, please wait to see your teachers at the front of the auditorium," Mrs. Gervis said.

There was an awkward pause once Mrs. Gervis finished speaking. Students seemed to have no idea what they should really be doing despite the direction given. Then, slowly at first, one by one they made their way out of the gymnasium and into the halls for the first classes of the day. Michael stood and entered the crowd making his way into the hall for his locker with Perminder, Carly, and Monica following swiftly behind.

"This is crazy. I wonder if Dave just stayed home to avoid the madness," Perminder said, once they got to the lockers.

"I'm sure we'll find out soon enough," Michael responded. The last thing he was trying to think about was Dave. Michael had been reluctant to tell Perminder how he had seen Dave once again being awfully chummy with Vince the night before.

"Okay, you two, we're off to class. We'll catch you at lunch?" Carly asked. She and Monica stood side by side with books in arm.

"I guess so, but who really knows what's going to happen around here today," Michael said.

Michael pretended to be rooting through his locker. He watched Carly and Monica vanish into the crowd. With the hall beginning to clear out, Michael motioned Perminder to follow as he headed for the bathroom just down the hall. As he stepped in, there was a boy washing his hands at the sink, but otherwise the room was empty. Michael stepped to a sink and began to wash his hands as well, waiting for the boy to finish and leave. Luckily, Perminder caught on and stopped at the sink against the wall and began to lean in and examine a pimple on his face closely. Finally the student left and they were alone and able to talk.

"Look, I need to get out of here. I have to go and find some answers so Titan can put a stop to all this," Michael said, turning off the faucet and began drying his hands.

"And just how do you plan on getting out of here unnoticed. In case you missed it, this place is on high alert right now," Perminder replied.

"I know how tight it is, and that's also how I know just how important it is that Titan get out of here to try and end this," Michael said, tossing his paper towel into the trash.

"Okay, let's just say that if you can get out of here, turn into Titan, and you could find this guy and stop all this crazy stuff. The problem is how do you transform and leave without anybody going 'oh hey isn't that Michael Novak that just turned into Titan and flew off?' I don't think that will help you in the long run."

"I know, and that's why I need to get to the roof. If I can get up there I can transform and leave without anybody noticing."

"Okay, I'm guessing you didn't tell Carly about any of this, am I right?"

"Carly would never understand the need to do this right now, but I need you to."

"So, how do you suggest we get you up to the roof?"

"The janitor room is right at the end of the hall. I know they have keys to the roof access in there. All I need from you is a diversion," Michael said, trying to look Perminder squarely in the eye. Perminder began to roll his eyes as Michael finished.

"What? You want me to stick my neck out and get in trouble so you can sneak off?"

"Hey, you'll be sticking your neck out in there, but I'll be sticking my neck out, out there," Michael said firmly, as he pointed through the wire meshed window that stood six feet off the ground.

"Fine, I'll do it. Just give me a minute here will ya?" Perminder groaned.

Michael said nothing as Perminder hopped in place a few times and shook his head and hands about wildly. Michael had seen him go through this same routine many times. It was what he always did before any big basketball or soccer game. Then, Perminder turned and opened the door.

"Once you get my signal you're all clear for at least a minute or two," Perminder said, turning back to Michael. "Maybe even longer, but a minute or two at least."

"Let me guess, I'll know the signal when I hear it," Michael said. Perminder said nothing in reply. He only smiled and then slipped through the bathroom door.

Michael waited anxiously in the middle of the boys' bathroom for Perminder's signal. Less than a minute later the fire alarm went off throughout the school. Michael smiled and exited the bathroom. He didn't look around at all. He simply marched, head down, toward the janitor's room at the end of the hall. He was nearly there when the first of the students began to enter the halls. He shifted into a quick walk, trying not to draw attention to himself. Suddenly, the hall was swarmed with students that were all going the opposite direction. Michael tried to go upstream, but soon he saw teachers usher students back the other way. He glanced down the length of the hall, and saw Mrs. Samuels standing in front of the janitor's room directing traffic. So, he turned, dejected, and followed the crowed back out the front doors.

Michael walked out onto the grass and started to move to the back quickly as students filed by to be accounted for. He saw many of the teachers out doing roll call. That's when he realized he had not gone to any class yet. With all the commotion going on, the only people that knew he was even at school were his friends, two of whom knew he was Titan. Michael stepped off the curb and then quickly ducked behind one of the blue vans parked there. He hadn't even seen Carly yet, so she wouldn't know he left until he missed lunch. Perminder had given him the perfect getaway. Michael casually turned, shoved his hands into his pockets and walked away, head down, without looking back.

Michael hadn't really thought about what to do next, he was mostly just going by the seat of his pants. All he knew at the moment was that he had to get far enough away from the school and be out of sight so that he could transform. Even after that he really didn't know what to do. He was hoping that Azure would have some idea.

Once he was a block from the school and he heard no one calling his name he knew he was clear. Now all he had to do was find a quiet place to transform. He walked another two blocks before he came across an alley that he was somewhat familiar with. He knew a lot of kids, such as friends of Vince, snuck back there to smoke at lunch hour. It was lined with high thick hedges that would conceal him nicely. He turned the corner toward the alley, and was grateful it was empty. It was clearly too early for any students to be here yet, he thought, not to mention the extra security at the school today. He knew he had just been lucky to get out undetected. He only hoped that Perminder hadn't been caught.

Michael walked up to the tallest part of the hedges and looked around just to be sure. He pulled out his cell phone and placed it on the ground. Best to stay connected to the world, he thought. Then he extended his right hand overhead and said the magic words.

"Exaudio Fortis!"

The blue lightning struck brilliantly, and as the smoke dissipated, Titan was left standing in the alley ready to hear from Azure.

"Azure, we have problems," Titan said.

I am aware that our shadowy nemesis struck again last night.

"Yeah, twice. The whole city is totally scared right now. Our school is in full lockdown. I was lucky to get out at all."

It is good that you did. We must do what we can to find this person. These attacks will likely only get worse. Many lives will be at stake.

"Well, where do you think we should start? I have no clue how to find this guy."

That's just it; we'll need to acquire clues. We need to start at one of the crime scenes from last night.

"Isn't that kind of risky? Both places are probably swarming with cops."

Yes, they likely are. You will need to use stealth and a great deal of caution so as not to alert them of our presence.

"Okay then, let's head to the theatre first. At least I know where that one is," Titan said, as he leaped into the air.

He soared to a four story building just down the street from Carly's. He was now high enough to get his bearings. From here he knew where the theatre was all too well. It was the same one where he had rescued Carly and Monica during his battle with Inferno.

Titan faced toward downtown and took three powerful strides before launching himself into the air toward the theatre. He soared high over the city slicing through the air, bandana and belt flapping in the wind behind him like a banner. Keeping concealed was not going to be easy.

He landed on a high-rise right next to the theatre. He cautiously made his way to the building's edge and peered down. The area in front of the theatre was still blocked off with police tape. Passers-by had to detour along the other side of the street as most of the sidewalk on the theatre side was blocked off. The regular day to day activity seemed to be at an all-time low. Very few people or passing cars were visible from the rooftop in any direction. Most of the activity that Titan could see came from the police below.

There were officers stationed right outside the theatre entrance and police cruisers at either end of the block. Titan moved along the side of the building until he was facing the back of the theatre. From there he saw two more officers at the rear entrance.

"Man, they have this place locked down good. I think I'm gonna just try and get to the roof and work my way inside to where the attack happened," Titan said.

That would be the best course of action. Just be careful. We don't know who will be inside, and should be ready for anything.

"Aren't I always careful?"

Perhaps we should ask your friend, Perminder.

"Oh, right, that. Look, that was just an accident. It was only Perminder, he would never tell anyone, I swear."

It is alright, but you are just lucky that it turned out to be your friend who saw you. What if it had been someone else? What if it had been your brother instead?

"I know I got lucky there. Message received. I'll be more careful. Now should I go?" Titan asked, as he prepared himself to leap to the theatre roof.

Yes, proceed.

Titan peered over the edge once more to ensure no one was watching. Then, he deftly leaped over the alleyway and onto the roof, trying to stay low and move as fast as he could. He rolled to a stop and stayed in a crouching position, waiting momentarily to see if any commotion followed his landing. When there was none, he made his way to the rooftop entrance.

There was a small doorway in the middle of the roof. Titan tried the handle once. It didn't budge. Bracing the door against his body, he grabbed the handle firmly with his other hand and pushed the door inward. The metal creaked as it bent with Titan's increasing pressure. Finally, it gave way and swung inward into darkness.

"How's that for careful? I barely made a sound opening that door, and it was solid steel."

Very good, but let us not get carried away with a simple door.

With a slight roll of his eyes, Titan walked into the dark passage. As his eyes adjusted he could see a set of stairs that led to another closed door with a crack of light seeping in from the bottom. Titan made his way down and put his ear to the door. When he heard nothing he tried the handle, this time it opened with ease, and he walked through.

Titan wove his way around the stacks of movie reels, confections, and paperwork boxes. He seemed to be in a storeroom. Nowhere did he see any sign of an attack. It must be contained to the main theatre itself, he thought. Through the main lobby, garbage and debris were strewn about showing the clear signs of a stampeding crowd making an emergency exit. Still seeing no signs of life, Titan went into the first of the three theatre rooms to look around.

Immediately, Titan could see the signs of the attack as he entered the first theatre. Chairs were torn and pulled from their floor bracing. The screen itself was shredded almost like some giant cat had gotten to it. People's personal effects had been left behind and littered the floor. As Titan continued to the front he saw that there were scorch marks on the surface of the walls, flooring and some of the seats at the front of the theatre.

Once Titan rounded the first row of seats, he saw a big dark hole about three feet in diameter that gaped between the front row and the screen. Titan crouched down to examine it, and saw what looked like dozens of claw marks down a long dark tunnel of cement and dirt that seemed to have no end.

"Wow, these things looked pretty vicious. It looks like they popped right out from under the ground here. This hole's not huge though, so they couldn't be all that big," Titan said, as he lowered his head as far down the narrow tunnel as he dared.

I agree, but there are no signs of what exactly attacked here. At least we know they came from underground and not above. It would be fair to assume that our enemy has a subterranean lair.

"Um yeah, that's what I was thinking too," Titan said, as he made mental note to ask Carly about the word subterranean later.

Suddenly the big double door leading from the lobby flew open and two plain clothes detectives and one uniformed officer stood in the doorway. They were in the middle of conversation when they came to an abrupt halt as they saw Titan standing at the front of the theatre. Titan recognized one of the detectives from the incident in the park when the police had chased him after the attack on the cargo ship last year.

"You, hold it right there!" Det. Langara shouted at Titan, reaching inside his jacket for his gun. The other officers broke from their trance and followed suit.

Titan responded by leaping up to the top of the stage and ducked under the remnants of the movie screen. He could hear the thunder of the officer's footfalls as they barreled down the aisle and tried to follow. Titan could hear one of them on the radio, trying to call for backup to other officers, no doubt waiting on the street.

You must get outside quickly or this will not end well. You must not get yourself captured.

"Okay, you're only giving information I already know about here," Titan said, as he carefully made his way through the darkened back of the theatre.

He could hear the police officers closing in fast. The sounds of doors slamming open and more footfalls could also be heard from the front of the theatre. He knew his paths of escape were being eliminated and quickly. Feeling along the wall at his right he rounded a corner and saw the welcomed glow of the red exit sign above a door.

Titan crashed through the door to the blinding sunlight of the alley behind the theatre. He could hear Det. Langara closing in behind him. He quickly pushed the door closed and grabbed hold of the edge of a dumpster next to it and pulled it in front of the exit, blocking it altogether. Titan glanced around and saw that two officers had come from around the front corner of the alley and started to draw their guns as they spotted Titan. Without hesitation he leaped back to the roof of the theatre.

"Okay, I think it's safe to say we've worn out our welcome here," Titan said as he peered over the rooftop and saw the flashing lights of more approaching police cruisers.

Agreed, it is time you made your getaway, and swiftly.

"Well, the good news is I have become very good at outrunning the police," Titan said sarcastically.

We need to avoid interaction with authorities at all costs. With the current situation the way it is, we do not want them to confuse your intentions with that of our latest enemy.

"No problem, I'll be outta here in a sec."

Titan stood and paced the length of the theatre rooftop. He broke into a run, focusing toward the east end. He leaped over to the next building and then up and over the next after that. He glanced down and saw a line of flashing police lights that seemed to be working its way down the street after him. Titan leaped higher and farther as he hit the edge of the last building putting two city blocks between him and the line of police cruisers following him. Once he landed, he took four powerful strides and launched himself into the air again. This time he sped virtually across the city and right into the middle of East Delta City. He landed in a full barrel roll on the roof of the Polson Park Mall, a place he knew far too well since it was the closest mall to his neighborhood.

"I think that should do it," Titan said, confidently, cocking his head back toward downtown trying to listen for an armada of police sirens.

Very good, I do believe this venture was fruitful. There is at least some information you have acquired about our enemy that we did not previously know. We can start looking for him right away.

"Yeah, and I need to get to Vicki too. I'm sure she's been looking into this as well."

Suddenly Titan felt his cell vibrate where it was tucked into his belt. He snatched it and saw unknown on the caller id. He paused then answered it anyway.

"Hello."

"Is this Michael Novak?"

"Yes, it is."

"I'm from Delta City General. I'm calling to inform you that your grandfather, Dale Novak, is being discharged and will need to be picked up."

"Thank you, I'll be there right away," Titan answered and then hung up. "Well, looks like the rest will have to be put on hold, Azure. I have to go pick up Grandpa Dale from the hospital."

Very well, we will reconvene later to discuss our next course of action.

"Sounds good," Titan said, as he was already holding his ring overhead. **"Extermino Fortis!"**

With wisps of smoke still clinging to him, Michael ran to the rooftop exit. He encountered no one, thankfully, so didn't have to explain why or how he had gotten to the roof. He ran all the way to the bus stop and waited as patiently as he could for the number twelve bus he knew would take him toward the hospital. Finally, the bus pulled up and Michael leaped up the stairs and in, dropping the few coins he had in his pocket as he went. The doors slammed close behind him. He swiftly moved half way down the aisle of the bus and sat in the window seat directly behind the driver. The driver put the bus in gear and they were off.

Michael sat in deep thought as the city rolled past him through the bus window. All he could think about after the last few days, was it would seem weird to have Grandpa Dale back at home. The thought actually gave him great comfort to think of how things used to be, and to know that his grandfather would be there waiting for him at home.

At last the bus pulled up in front of the hospital. Two orderlies were standing in front of Grandpa Dale who was sitting slumped in a wheel chair. Michael couldn't help but think how weak his grandfather looked. He was still not accustomed to seeing him this way. Grandpa Dale had been blind Michael's whole life, but never in a physically weakened condition.

"Hi, Grandpa," Michael said, bounding down the bus steps to greet him.

"Hello, son," Grandpa Dale replied.

"I hope they haven't had you waiting out here for very long."

"Not too long. Besides, I just wanted some fresh air. I knew you wouldn't be too long."

"Are you ready to go?" Michael asked. He was actually just relieved that Titan's business had not kept him any longer than it had.

"Son, I've been ready to go for the last three days."

Michael reached down and grabbed hold of Grandpa Dale's hand and helped him rise out of the chair. One of the orderlies pulled the chair away. Grandpa Dale took a second to steady himself and then stood straight up.

"Are you two going to be okay then?" one of the orderlies asked.

"Oh, I think we'll be just fine thank you," Grandpa Dale replied.

The two orderlies turned and walked back to the front entrance of the hospital.

"Does my chariot await?" Grandpa Dale asked, breaking into a smile.

"Yeah, this is a bus loop so it's still here and ready for us."

"Well then, what are we just standing around here for?"

Michael held on to Grandpa Dale's arm as he took the first step up into the bus. The bus driver didn't even look at them and instead was scrolling through his smart phone. By the time Grandpa Dale had reached the top step, he seemed out of breath and exhausted. Michael quickly leaped up the few stairs to help his grandfather to the nearest seat. Grandpa Dale felt around the seats to gain an understanding of his surroundings and then plopped into the bench behind the driver with a loud sigh.

The driver slid the bus into gear and it rumbled down the road and began to weave its way back to the east side. Michael's attention was equally drawn to the wellbeing of Grandpa Dale and the scenes passing by the window to his left. Police and military vehicles were parked at most major intersections. Barricades were set up across certain roads in an attempt by authorities to control what traffic was on the road. Michael put his right hand over his left and rubbed the ring with the small blue jewel on his index finger. His desire to transform and face the city as Titan had never been greater, but he knew he would simply have to wait for now.

Suddenly Michael felt his phone buzz in his pocket and he pulled it out, flipped it open and saw a text from Perminder. He thought twice about opening it at first. He felt he had set his friend up to get in trouble, and wasn't sure he wanted to hear about the fallout. The last thing he felt like getting was grief from Perminder about whatever trouble he was in. Then, he finally hit view and read the message.

THANKS FOR THAT
I'M IN DETENTION FOR TWO WEEKS NOW THANKS TO YOU.
YOU OWE ME BIG TIME!

Michael smiled after reading the message. Then he hit reply and began typing a response.

I KNOW. I AM SORRY BUD.
YOU WEREN'T SUPPOSED TO GET CAUGHT!
I WILL TOTALLY LET YOU DO SOMETHING COOL
WITH MY STAFF NEXT TIME I TRANSFORM!

Michael knew the way to satisfy Perminder was to give him a chance to handle any bit of Titan power that he could. Suddenly, his phone buzzed again.

DEAL!!!!!

Michael smiled and closed his phone and shoved it back into his pocket. Twenty-five minutes later the bus pulled up just down the road from the little white house where Michael and Grandpa Dale lived. Once the bus came to a stop, Grandpa Dale slowly slid to the edge of the seat and reached out until he found the top corners and pulled himself to his feet. Michael remained poised, ready to help whenever he was needed, with an arm extended carefully to help his grandpa balance. Grandpa Dale's feet slid and felt their way down the narrow aisle. Twice the toe of one of his shoes caught the base of the seats. Before he could trip, Michael was right there to steady him.

Going down the steps proved far trickier for Grandpa Dale. It was then that Michael realized they had left the house and gone to the hospital without taking his cane. It was the first time that Michael had ever seen him leave the house without it. Once his foot hit the sidewalk Grandpa Dale's stride seemed to grow more confident. Michael turned to smile to the bus driver, and as the doors slammed shut, the bus slipped back into gear and it roared off down the road.

Slowly the two made their way down the block to home. Grandpa Dale took careful shuffling steps. Michael, meanwhile, held firmly to his arm, guiding and supporting his grandfather.

They entered the yard, and it seemed Michael was the one struggling to keep up. Sight or no sight, Grandpa Dale knew his way around the house and yard. Michael raced ahead so he could unlock the door. Grandpa Dale walked confidently down the cement walkway in the yard. Once Michael got up the few steps and to the door he found that it was already opened. He wanted to think that he had forgotten to lock it, but was sure he had. The door then suddenly swung open, and Vince was standing there to greet them.

"Hi, Grandpa, glad to see you home so soon," Vince said. "Sorry I couldn`t be there to get you with Michael, but I was busy with work."

"That's alright, Vince, I understand," Grandpa Dale said, as he started up the steps.

Vince held the door open and moved aside as Grandpa Dale and Michael came through the back entrance and into the kitchen. Grandpa Dale moved slowly but sure footedly to his usual chair at the kitchen table and sat down. He was panting heavily and his hands were shaking slightly. Just as Michael moved in to see if he was alright, the cell in Vince's pocket dinged. Michael watched him out of the corner of his eye step out the back door.

"Are you okay, Grandpa?" Michael asked, leaning over him, clearly concerned.

"Oh, I think that ride back just zapped my energy, that's all," Grandpa Dale replied.

"Well, maybe you should listen to your doctor's orders and go have a rest," Michael suggested. "It's going to take a bit of time for you to get back to full strength."

"Maybe I'll just go relax in my chair and listen to the news," Grandpa Dale said. Michael knew that meant he could expect him to be asleep in mere minutes.

"Okay, you want me to help you get there?"

"That's alright, I think I've got it from here," Grandpa Dale said, starting to rise.

Michael heard Vince's voice on the back steps, but could make out none of what he was saying. He stood by, prepared to help if needed, as Grandpa Dale finished getting to his feet. Once he was up, Grandpa Dale shuffled his feet into the living room and fell back into his old easy chair. The foot rest went up and Grandpa Dale flicked on the radio at the little table beside the chair. Michael stood in the doorway to the living room for several seconds and then went to the back door.

Michael slowly opened the back door, trying to be inconspicuous and seeing if he could hear Vince's conversation. He spotted Vince right away at the bottom of the back steps with his back to him. He was still talking on the phone. Michael quietly stepped outside and closed the back screen door behind him.

"Okay, I'll be there in ten minutes," Vince said, and then hung up and pocketed the phone.

"What, you're just going to take off?" Michael snapped as soon as Vince turned around.

"You spying on me, runt?" Vince snapped back. "'Cause, I'll tell you one thing right now, it's none of your business what I do."

"I personally could not really care less, but for some reason Grandpa does care about you. The way I see it, since you were pretty much the one that sent him to the hospital you should stay a little while and make sure he's okay," Michael said, his voice rising with each word.

Without knowing, Michael's hands had clenched into tight fists. He took one step down toward Vince. At first Vince seemed slightly taken aback by Michael's defiance. His eyes had popped wide open and he stepped back slightly as Michael had stepped forward. Suddenly, his eyes narrowed and an angry sneer spread across his lips.

"Is that it? You think I'm the one who put him there?" Vince seethed.

"You'd be surprised how much I know about you, Vince. Like, the car parked over by the cemetery. Or even about your job with good old Dylan Thompson."

Michael was running on pure emotion. He felt all kinds of rage that had been building up suddenly coming to the surface. His heart was pounding like a jackhammer. He only hoped Vince wouldn't notice the slight tremor that had spread through both his arms and hands. He seemed unable to control just what would come out in his tirade. His only thoughts were a single focus on trying to not mention anything about Titan. Vince's eyebrows grew narrower with Michael's revelations. His clenched lips were all but invisible. Then, he broke into his old wolfish grin.

"You say that about my job like it's such a bad thing. Funny, your old buddy Dave sure doesn't seem to think so. Why don't you ask him? Pretty soon he may just be working for me."

"Shut up!" Michael shouted.

"What? I can't help that your buddy wants to make some cash with me."

Michael launched himself off the steps and collided with Vince. The force knocked them both over backward, but Michael had managed to maintain his position on top of Vince. He began throwing wild punches. Then, Vince broke one muscular arm free and threw a vicious cross that landed against Michael's mouth.

Michael was sent toppling over. His upper lip had exploded into sharp bursts of pain. He tasted copper as a trickle of blood ran down his lips. Michael rolled over and tried to get to his feet when a large shadow loomed over them.

"You're dead now, runt," Vince said in a low voice, crouching directly over Michael.

Without even thinking Michael shot his right leg up between Vince's legs. Vince doubled over with his hands pressed to his midsection. Michael got to his knees grabbed Vince by the shirt collar and cocked his right hand back ready to strike.

"Michael!" Grandpa Dale yelled from the back door. "What's going on out here?"

The brothers both froze tangled up in the middle of the back lawn.

"Nothing, Grandpa, just horseplay," Michael said, as he gave Vince a final shove that sent him face first into the grass.

"Michael, get in here now," Grandpa Dale said. Michael noticed right away that he was shaky and pale and somewhat wheezy.

"Coming."

Michael sulked to the steps and went inside. As he reached the door he looked back to see Vince trying to get back to his feet with one hand still clutching just below his waist. Michael was unable to restrain the grin from his face as he went to the kitchen table and sat down.

"Grandpa, that wasn't what it seemed like," Michael said as soon as he sat down.

"I may be blind, but I'm not stupid," Grandpa Dale responded, making his way back to the table. "You don't think I can tell the sound of you boys fighting in the backyard?"

Michael saw Grandpa Dale's brow furrowed in anger for the first time in a long time. He also seemed very weak and ready to collapse. His body heaved with his heavy breathing. Michael instantly felt guilty knowing that the last thing his grandpa needed was added stress, or another trip to the hospital. Michael then heard the back gate slam as Vince undoubtedly had stormed off. He had no idea what the repercussions would be from the fight, but it was likely not to be good for him.

"I'm sorry, Grandpa. I just get so mad when I see the disrespect that Vince shows you. I mean, he's the one that practically put you in the hospital," Michael said, grateful to have finally been able to say it aloud to Grandpa Dale.

Michael watched intently as Grandpa Dale pulled out a chair and sat down. He said nothing at first; he only sat there with his hands resting on the table. His cane stood by the door as he rarely used it once inside the house.

"I think it's time I tell you what I told Vince on the day I had my heart attack. It may just help you think a little differently about your brother. I only hope it doesn't make you think any different about myself," Grandpa Dale said in a calm voice, lower than Michael had ever heard him speak.

"I have wanted to tell both of you for some time, but I felt that the time had to be right. I wanted you both to be mature enough to handle it."

Michael leaned in close, ready to listen. His mind was racing, his body on edge as he tried to prepare for what Grandpa Dale was about to say.

"As I already said, I'm no fool. I know full well what kind of trouble Vince is likely up to, and the kinds of people he runs with in this neighborhood. I only told him first because he was older, and I thought maybe it would help convince him to get back on the right track with his life. You see, Michael, I feel I've failed Vince. I've let him somehow sour and turn to bad things to get by. I only ever wanted to help him, raise him right, like your parents would have wanted."

"Grandpa, that's just not true. You've always been there for the both of us. Why are you accepting responsibility for his actions? Vince is up to no good because he is just no good," Michael quickly interjected.

Grandpa Dale was shaking his head slowly back and forth.

"You're different Michael, but Vince still remembers so much of the time just before your parents died. It has left a lasting impression on him. That's why I told him first, but it's time to tell you now. Your parents didn't just die in a car accident, Michael. They were killed!"

It seemed as though time had stood still once the words were said. Michael was frozen; his mouth hung ajar, his eyes wide. It felt like he had just been hit in the chest with a sledgehammer. He had never even thought to think of his parent's death in any other way besides an accident. To hear that they had been killed shocked him to the core.

"I know you've heard many of the stories about all the great things your parents did for the neighborhood. They were integral in keeping this neighborhood intact for many years. Your father worked constantly through city hall to fight for this neighborhood. Your mother was a common fixture at his side, when she wasn't working full time, here amongst us. It was all that great work that ended up putting a target on their backs. Before he died, your father told me all about the information he was gathering on, Mr. Midnight, and the threat he posed to this place."

Michael felt a chill run up his spine at the very mention of the name.

"It seemed your father had done some research of his own as city alderman, and was ready to take his information to the police. In fact, he had mentioned Chief Ross as one of the officers he was working with; of course he wasn't chief back then. He felt that even though he couldn't prove who Mr. Midnight was, he could prove that he existed and ran a vast majority of the Delta City criminal network. Your father believed that much of the criminal network was about to make its home in our neighborhood."

Grandpa Dale paused. He lowered his head and brought his hands down to his lap. Michael could have sworn he saw his chin quiver, though his voice never wavered.

"It seems that he was getting a little too close to something, and he was meddling too deep in unsavory waters. I know the car your parents drove and how Kevin looked after it. There was no way they just drove off the road like that from failed brakes. Your father was an excellent driver. I don't need to see to know that. You can feel a bad driver when you ride with one. It seemed the car was tampered with. The brake lines were cut while they were at a fund raiser. Every time the investigation was elevated however, it was derailed. Evidence was lost. Witnesses went missing. Finally the case was dropped and listed as accidental. It was largely believed by everyone from the neighborhood, to city hall, to Ross and the DCPD, however, that they died at the hands of Mr. Midnight's organization."

Michael was speechless. A million thoughts swirled through his head.

"How can that be? Why would they drop the case?" Michael asked at last, unable to hide the emotion in his voice.

"People were scared. The only one who was defiantly standing up to the corruption and crime of Mr. Midnight openly was your father and he had just died. Ross tried his best to carry on the investigation, but no one would stand at his side any longer. They didn't want to end up with the same fate as your parents," Grandpa Dale replied, his own voice now cracking with emotion even after all these years.

"They're gone from Vince and me because they were fighting for the greater good?" Michael asked, rhetorically.

"Michael, you must know they were fighting so tirelessly because of the both of you. They wanted to know that their sons would be safe in this city, and they were willing to fight against its worst criminals in order to make that a possibility. Everyone else was simply too scared to join them. "

Michael stood and went to his grandpa. He wrapped his arms around the old man's shoulders and rested his cheek against the top of his head.

"Thank you for telling me all of this, Grandpa," he whispered.

Michael felt Grandpa Dale's hands meet his own and squeeze.

"I'm just sorry it took this long for you to find out," Grandpa Dale stated.

Michael helped Grandpa Dale back into the living room and into his easy chair. He waited and watched as he drifted off to sleep within minutes. He then went to his room and lay on his bed staring at the ceiling for hours, lost in an ocean of his own thoughts. He didn't hear Vince come home that night.

CHAPTER 9: Pieces of the Puzzle

"Michael, I don't know what to say," Carly said, as Michael had finished telling her and Perminder all that had happened the day before.

The three of them were sitting on Carly's rooftop. They had planned to meet up and enjoy the bright beautiful afternoon that lay before them. Of course the current tensions all over the city had made that quite difficult. All three of them were very nearly banned from leaving their homes. They were able to meet on the rooftop, their usual place, but getting anywhere else was proving quite challenging. Monica's parents had refused to let her leave the house for the entire except for school. Dave had been unable to be reached for two days, which suited Michael's needs just fine. He needed to be able to talk to Perminder and Carly about Titan business.

"You don't really think that Vince and Dave could be working for Mr. Midnight do you?" Perminder asked. Michael was also able to get Perminder caught up on all his suspicions about his brother and friend.

"Well, I'm pretty sure about Vince. I did catch him at that warehouse when I faced off against Midnight, when they had the motion inhibitor. And Dave, well, if he works for either Vince or Dylan Thompson then he is connected to Mr. Midnight one way or the other," Michael responded.

"I just can't get past that. We're so tight with Dave, how could he do that?" Perminder asked.

"Let's not jump to too many conclusions until we know about Dave for sure," Carly said.

"True, let's just all act normal around him until we know anything. You should all have no problem. I'm the one who just learned that one of my best friends may be working for the man who evidently killed my parents," Michael stated. Carly grimaced at the words and Perminder turned his head down to his feet.

"Unfortunately, as bad as the possibility of our friend working for Mr. Midnight is, I think the bigger problem is the guy who has the entire city under his thumb right now. You need to figure how to put an end to that threat," Carly said to Michael.

"Well, I think the best thing to do right now is for me to go to Vicki and see what information she has on all of this," Michael said.

"Right now, in broad daylight?" Perminder asked.

"I don't think I really have a choice. I need to get this whole mess wrapped up as soon as possible," Michael responded.

"What about the laws and the curfew?" Perminder asked.

"I think I can work around that," said Michael

Michael stood and held his right hand in front of himself and closed it tightly into a fist and raised it high overhead.

"What, you're gonna change right now?" Perminder asked.

"Well, I don't see any point in waiting," Michael responded.

Michael took several steps back and glanced around quickly. Perminder only stared in wide-eyed disbelief. Carly did him the favor of covering his eyes with her other hand.

"Exaudio Fortis!"

The blast engulfed Michael and he instantly felt the surge of energy course through his body. As smoke dissipated all around him he saw Perminder and Carly both still sitting before him with her arms raised to shield themselves from the blast.

"Whoa! I don't know if I'll ever get used to seeing that," Perminder said, soaking in the transformation Michael had just undergone.

"Join the club," Carly whispered at him.

"Okay, so I'm off to find out about our shadowy villain then. With luck I can have this thing wrapped up by tomorrow. Wish me luck," Titan said.

"Okay, good luck. We'll catch up with you later," Carly said.

Titan stepped to the rooftop ledge. He glanced back and saw Carly and Perminder now standing and staring at him. He almost hated to leave them, but he knew the fate of the city could likely be resting in his hands. He got his bearings and then leaped forward. When he saw the city spread out below him he knew he had to land as quickly as he could.

He landed on top of a ten story apartment building at the edge of the east side. He gazed out over the city and took in what he saw. There were two military helicopters hovering over the city; one over the downtown area and the other over the harbor. He was also barely able to make out all of the barricades across many roads throughout the city. According to the news, Police were attempting to control access of civilians through the city.

Why have we landed? Are we not going to see the reporter?

"There are far too many cops and military out there. I think I really need to lay low. It'll just take us a little longer to get there. I'm going to keep low, and try to stay out of sight," Titan answered.

Very well, that sounds like the best course of action.

"But…I mean, okay then. Let's go!" said Titan, surprised.

Titan had expected Azure to disagree with him instantly. He was, however, relieved to have him agree with his decision. It felt like having one of his teachers at school validate a right answer in front of the whole class.

Titan tried to stay low and against the walls and ledges. When he took to the air he jumped in a direct line from one building to another. He was only taking enough air to land safely. The leaps were shorter but effective. The only bad part was he was unable to see where the helicopters had gotten.

All seemed to be going well. He was even making relatively good time as he had just crossed the halfway point to Vicki's office. He landed on the roof of a high rise apartment building just as one of the two military helicopters rounded a corner directly ahead of him. Luckily, Titan had seen the helicopter with just enough time to land and then roll and tuck himself behind the stairwell entrance.

He could see the helicopter's shadow, and felt the wind kick up as it swooped around, turning abruptly toward him. Titan instantly pulled himself against the wall and quickly moved to the far side and out of sight of the helicopter. It drew closer and hovered just overhead. Titan crouched down and moved to the far corner of the stairwell structure.

"Okay, so much for staying out of sight," Titan said.

Do not be hasty. Try to remain still and have patience. If they spot you, or if another helicopter approaches, we will decide another course of action then.

"Don't worry; I'm in no hurry to tangle with one of those things."

Titan was able to watch the helicopter's shadow as it swung to the left and began to do a search of the rooftop perimeter. He was finally able to put himself on the opposite side of the entryway them Titan made his move. He ran for the ledge and slid as he got closer to the edge. He then dropped down and was able to fall to a window ledge two stores down. He shuffled his way into the building's corner, out of sight from the helicopter. From there he waited and listened. He wasn't even aware that he had been holding his breath most of the time until he gasped and had to take in a fresh breath of air. Finally he heard the helicopter's engine rev higher and then saw it rise and fly back toward the harbor.

"Okay, that was too close for comfort. I think I might be taking the bus home," Titan said.

That was quick thinking, Titan. It was very good work.

Titan couldn't help but crack a smile at the compliment. He eased himself out of the corner and resumed his journey. His level of caution remained high, yet he was able to make it the rest of the way without incident. He touched down onto the rooftop of the Courier offices and dropped himself down to Vicki's window ledge much as he had just done while evading the helicopter. He peered inside and saw her busy going through information on her computer, the hand on her mouse scrolling and clicking away furiously. He tapped on the window gently. Vicki jumped slightly and swung her chair around to the window. She threw the window open and Titan entered. Vicki took a few steps back as he entered. Vicki then quickly ran over and locked the office door from inside and closed the blinds by the door that led into the currently empty hallway.

"I was starting to wonder when I would see you again," Vicki said, turning back to face him. "I didn't think it would be daytime though, especially considering all the added security around the city right now. Hopefully you had no trouble getting here."

"Well, it's been easier, but I made it. I just didn't think this should wait. There is, after all, pretty good reason for this security. I want to put an end to all this right away. I saw no point in waiting," Titan said, as he tried to keep an eye out the window for one of the hovering helicopters.

"Well, I'm glad you're here. Looks as though I've missed some pretty big stories lately, care to fill me in?"

Titan spent the next several minutes telling Vicki about his battles with both Sonic and Hawk. He was sure not to leave out any detail regarding the military involvement either. He even told her about the brief faceoff he'd had with Chief Ross and his men during the battle with Hawk. Vicki was making quick notes on her computer at rapid pace as he told his story.

"I'm just sorry I wasn't able to be there when those robots attacked the other night," Titan said. Vicki then told him about the meeting she had with Det. Langara.

She continued, "This threat seems to be serious alright. I got word from a member of city hall who's quite reliable that the military are not just here by coincidence. It seems that a former member of their ranks has gone rogue and set up a little army of his own, whom I can only assume is the one behind all of this. They have been tracking him for years. It just so happens that they tracked him to Delta City right when all these attacks started. So, you can relax, they're definitely not here for you. At least they're not here for you right now. They've come to clean up some of their own mess. My source says the mastermind behind all of this is a guy named Dr. Karl Melodian. I did a little research of my own and discovered he was a former military scientist and research developer. By all accounts the guy is a major genius. He's probably one of the three smartest people on the planet. Unfortunately, he just happens to have lost his grip on sanity. He was discharged from the military about five years ago and has only resurfaced in the last three years. So far he's posed no real threat, but, you just know that the military isn't keeping tabs on him for no reason. I have no idea about the real background or identification for either Sonic or Hawk. They're probably nothing more than low level flunkies that Melodian has brought in to his new organization."

"Any leads as to where he may be exactly?" Titan asked.

"Sorry, that's kind of where my leads ran dry. There's nothing on the guy for the present. All I could find was his past. He has to be somewhere in the city limits to orchestrate an attack like this, but unfortunately it's kind of a big city," Vicki said.

"Weren't the big screen messages he set up able to be traced somehow?" asked Titan.

"Like I said, the guy is a major genius. No one's been able to crack those. I've heard they aren't even able to be replayed by either the police or the military. That's how smart and sophisticated this guy's designs are. I'm told that he can literally create anything from any mechanical device he gets his hands on. I mean, you saw how advanced Sonic and Hawk were right?" Vicki asked.

"Oh, I saw all right," Titan replied.

"Can you imagine what he could do with an army of either of those? Have you even thought about what he might have in store for us next?" Vicki queried.

"I have, and that's why I'm here. I need to find him and stop him now," Titan said.

"Have you thought about going to Chief Ross?" she asked him.

"You just finished telling me how he had one of his men come here trying to get you to turn me in. So, why would I do that?" Titan asked in return.

"I know what I said, but I also know a good man when I see one, and I'm telling you Chief Ross is a good man. I think if you were able to get him alone and talk to him you might be able to reason with him. Then, you could work with him instead of having him trying to catch you," Vicki said.

Grandpa Dale's story about his father and Chief Ross suddenly came to mind. It would definitely be something to think about, but not just yet.

"I'll consider it, but I gotta say I'm really in no rush to stick my neck out any more than it already is. Anyway, I better get going; I have a bad guy to find," said Titan.

"Titan, just wait," pleaded Vicki. "I forgot to tell you about the guy who's here to capture Dr. Melodian. His name is General Stevenson. From all I've heard he is one serious customer, kind of a take-no-prisoner type.

So, just be careful. He may not be here to take you in, but that doesn't mean he won't plough through you to get to Melodian, okay?"

"Okay, thanks. I'll be careful and keep my eyes peeled for him," Titan responded.

Titan stepped onto the window ledge. He looked around cautiously for one of the helicopters and once he saw that the coast was clear he prepared to jump. He glanced back once at Vicki, smiled and nodded. Then, he leaped forward to the roof of the adjacent building. He sprung over six more buildings until he was a good dozen blocks away from Vicki's office. He was careful to stay low and always had a watchful eye out for helicopters. He decided not to press his luck any further and dropped down into the alley of the midtown building he was standing on.

"Well, Azure, at least we know a little bit about our enemy," Titan said, once he landed in the alley.

Yes, now we will have to formulate a plan, and quickly. We still do not know when or where this Dr. Melodian will strike again.

"I'm going to transform and head back home. From there I'm going to see what I can look up and research myself from my computer with Carly's help. By nightfall it will be much safer to come out and I can start to really search for this guy," Titan said.

He glanced around the alley to make sure he wasn't being watched and then said the magic words.

"Extermino Fortis!"

Once he was back to plain old Michael Novak he walked down the alley and peered out into the street. He was in what was usually a busy part of the city. Currently, due to the fear and restrictions, there was hardly anyone around. Just as he was starting to wonder how he was going to get home, he saw a lone city bus turn the corner and come lumbering up the street toward him. Michael stepped out onto the sidewalk and was relieved to see no police or military personnel. He wasn't' even sure if he would get in trouble if he was caught out in this part of the city at this time of day right now. He was very grateful to see the bus stop sign. The bus hissed to a stop and its doors flung open. Michael stepped inside and dropped some change into the meter and took a seat. There was only one other person on the bus with him.

"Where you headed?" the driver asked as he turned back to Michael.

"Um… the east side, around King James and one twentieth," Michael replied spouting off the nearest main intersection to his neighborhood.

"Great, it's on my way. I'm supposed to take people wherever they need to go until this whole thing blows over. So, unless someone else hops in, you're my second stop of the afternoon," the driver said to Michael.

"Ah, don't worry, man. Titan will catch this fool and then things will be back to normal," the other passenger chimed in.

"Yeah, I hear that," the driver responded. "I hope Titan catches that guy and gets him but good."

Michael turned to the window. He couldn't help but smile at the remark. It made him feel good to know that someone in the city believed in Titan at least. It also did nothing but remind him that he currently had no idea how he was going to stop Dr. Melodian. He sat dwelling on these two conflicting emotions until the bus at last pulled up to his stop. Once the bus came to a stop he got up and made his way for the door.

Michael stepped off and turned toward home with his head hung down and his hands jammed deep into his pockets. As he approached the Burger Pit, he saw a familiar face and decided to go over.

"Hey, Dave, what are you doing here?" Michael asked.

He found Dave leaning up against the front of the restaurant looking down at his feet.

"What, you always telling me who I can hang out with now you wanna tell me where I can hang out?" Dave spat back.

"Whoa, I never said anything like that. What's wrong with you?" Michael shot back.

"You've been nothing but a jerk to me ever since I started talking to your brother. The way I see it you're the one with something wrong, not me," Dave declared.

"Oh, so now you want to acknowledge the fact that you've been hanging with Vince, a guy we all know is a low life."

"Well, that low life just offered me a job working with him down at the docks after school and on weekends."

Michael could feel the words he had ready suddenly jam in his throat. He stammered silently for a moment and then continued.

"Did you say job? You have a job with Vince?" Michael asked at last.

"Yeah, that's right. This is a great opportunity too. My family could really use this money, so, I'm gonna be seeing a lot more of Vince. You're just going to have to make a choice here, you'll have to either accept me associating with your brother or we just may not be able to be friends anymore," Dave said.

Michael watched in stunned silence as Dave turned and walked down the end of the block and then vanished around the corner. Michael stood there in the middle of the sidewalk, brooding, for some time before finally heading home himself.

CHAPTER 10: Hammerhead

"Well, it's been some time, I think, since we all had a meal together," Grandpa Dale said, as he sat at the side of the kitchen table.

It was Monday afternoon and Michael, Grandpa Dale, and Vince were all having a late afternoon lunch in the house. The only one who spoke the whole time was Grandpa Dale. Vince and Michael simply hovered low over the table eating their sandwich while they glared at each other silently. It was the first time they had been in the same room since their fight three days ago. And it seemed Grandpa Dale had orchestrated the whole thing. He had gotten Vince to get him a travel pass, which was now required to get through the city for an appointment at a clinic at the edge of downtown. The passes had become mandatory for any movement throughout the city that was not already authorized. He had then asked Michael to take him to the appointment as soon as his classes let out.

"Yeah, this is great," Vince said, sarcastically through a mouthful of sandwich.

"Did you get the pass, Vince?" Grandpa Dale asked, before Michael could say anything.

"Yes, it's on the table beside your chair, remember?" said Vince.

"Oh, that's right," Grandpa Dale replied.

"I gotta run. I have to be at work soon," Vince said, getting up and taking his plate to the sink.

"Say 'hi' to Dave for me," Michael seethed.

Vince turned from the sink and stared at Michael with an evil grin, one that no villain he had faced as Titan had topped yet.

"Oh, I will, and why don't you do me a favour, when you see your buddy, Perminder, let him know if he's looking for work to give me a call too."

Michael gritted his teeth and clenched his hands into tight fists on top of the table. If Grandpa Dale hadn't been there the two likely would have started fighting again right there in the kitchen. Before Michael could say anything else, Vince turned and went out the back door. Michael didn't so much as flinch until he heard the back gate slam shut. When Michael turned back to Grandpa Dale, he couldn't help but feel guilty as he saw the solemn look in his grandfather's face. Grandpa Dale's head hung low and shook slowly from side to side.

"Well, I guess I'll finish getting ready to go," Michael said, as he began to make his way to the bathroom.

"I just wish you two boys could get along," Grandpa Dale said suddenly.

Michael paused and winced at the words. His hands reached out and grabbed the edges of the doorway. He slowly turned back toward his grandpa, but could think of nothing to say.

"You two are brothers. Nothing will ever change that. I won't be around forever, you know. You both need to be there for one another, to help each other if necessary. Soon, you'll both be the only family that either of you have left," Grandpa Dale continued.

Once he was finished he carefully stood and began to walk toward the living room with his right hand extended for guidance. Michael stepped aside to let him pass. His bottom jaw moved slowly up and down as he struggled to find the right words to respond, yet none came.

Michael blurted at last, "Grandpa, I'm sorry. I try not to let Vince bother me, but when I see how his actions affect those I care about, I just can't help myself."

"I know, son. Perhaps this is the time that he would need your guidance. Just because you're the younger brother doesn't mean you can't offer advice," Grandpa Dale responded, managing the faintest of smiles. "I'm going to go call the cab."

Michael opened his mouth to say more, but no words were forthcoming. He assumed Grandpa Dale knew about at least some of the bullying Michael had endured at the hands of Vince over the years. It was one thing to point out the lack of respect Vince showed anyone, but it was another to tell of the crimes he was sure he had witnessed Vince take part in as Titan. He wanted to tell his grandfather so badly, but he couldn't bear the thought of causing him more anguish, even to expose Vince as the criminal he truly believed his brother had become.

Michael watched Grandpa Dale shuffle into the living room and grab the phone by his arm chair. As his grandfather's words began to sink in, he walked down the hall to the bathroom and finished getting ready. Once he was finished and walked back into his bedroom he heard his cell buzzing on his night table. He quickly checked the display, flipped it open and answered.

"Hey, Perminder."

"Mike, I was thinking maybe we could head along the shoreline and see if we could spot where Sonic and Hawk came from. I was looking online at the areas of their attacks and there are a couple places that cross. Those could be your leads to finding this Melodian guy."

Michael, Carly, and Perminder had spent a good two hours checking information online at Carly's the night before. It hadn't led to anything substantial, but it had given Perminder a few ideas about where to start looking for Dr. Melodian.

"That sounds like a good idea, really it does, but I have to go with my grandpa to one of his doctor appointments. I'll call you after though, okay?"

"Oh yeah, sure, no problem." Michael could hear the disappointment in his friend's voice. "If you want, I can go snoop around a little while you're gone. I can kinda give you the full report later so you can check it out, you know."

"Don't even think about it. First, I don't think it's wise that you go poking around the docks or anything all on your own. Second of all, what if one of your ideas does lead to Melodian and Titan can't be there to help you?" Michael asked. "I appreciate you wanting to help me out, but I don't need you tempting fate like that."

"Fine, but I am gonna keep checking stuff online. See what else I can dig up there. Is that okay, or is that too dangerous too?" Perminder said, clearly disappointed.

"Don't pull the 'hard done by' routine with me. I'm just trying to stop you from getting yourself killed. I gotta run. I'll call you later."

Michael clasped his phone shut and stuffed it in his jean's pocket as he glimpsed the time, and realized he was quickly running out of it. He rushed over to his dresser to grab his wallet and was frozen in place when he caught a glimpse of a familiar old photograph on top of his dresser. It was one of the last taken of his whole family together. Young Michael and Vince sat cross legged in a park with their parents proud and smiling crouched behind. Usually it was the image of his parents that caught his attention from the photo, but this time it was something different. He looked at himself in the photo, and he wasn't looking straight ahead or even back at his parents. He was looking over at his big brother. Looking at that younger image of Vince, Michael felt something for his brother that he hadn't in ages, love and adoration, as he thought of how he used to feel toward him.

"Michael, are you ready?" Grandpa Dale called out from the kitchen.

Michael was quickly snapped back to reality. He placed the photo in his top drawer and went to the kitchen.

"Coming," he called out as he went down the hall.

The cab was waiting out front. Michael helped his grandfather down the back steps and around to the front of the house. He got the feeling the

Grandpa Dale was disappointed and upset with him for fighting with Vince, but hoped he was wrong. They both climbed into the back of the cab.

"You have a travel pass?" the driver asked.

"Yes, of course," Grandpa Dale responded, handing the driver the orange card from his jacket pocket.

The driver inspected it then nodded his head and handed it back. Grandpa Dale once again pocketed it and rested his hand back over his cane which was laid across his lap. Without another word the cab began to roll forward leaving their house, and then the eastside behind them as it moved uptown toward the hospital where the appointment was, at a nearby clinic.

Michael's cell pinged with an incoming text message. He pulled out his phone and flipped it open. It was Carly saying that Perminder had shown up at her home wanting her to go with him to some location in search of Hawk and Sonic. Michael's thumb flew over his key pad furiously telling her to keep him away no matter what. He loved that he didn't have to lie to Perminder anymore , but his new found enthusiasm for helping was starting to prove much more of a hindrance than aid so far. Carly responded that she would do her best. He knew that meant that there was no way that Perminder would get anywhere near the borders of the eastside. He leaned back, relieved and looked over at his grandpa.

Usually conversation was easy between Michael and his grandpa, but today he found it harder than he ever had before. He had never tried so hard while coming up empty. Grandpa Dale simply sat facing forward unmoving, almost statuesque. Michael, on the other hand, couldn`t stop fidgeting. He tried to occupy himself with the view of the city that was going by, but to no avail. He was able to note, however, that it was quite strange that he really had seen the city so many times in the last several months, but it has always been by air while he was leaping and bounding over the city. At last the cab pulled up to a five story office building three blocks away from the hospital.

"Okay, here we are. That'll be seventeen fifty," the driver said as he slipped the cab in park at the curb in front.

Michael paid the driver while Grandpa Dale got out of the cab carefully leading with his cane. Michael came around to his grandpa once out of the cab himself. Grandpa Dale had one hand on his cane and the other through Michael's arm for extra support. He was surprisingly sure-footed for a blind man in areas he was familiar with at home or in the neighborhood, but this was an entirely new area. It was just as well that Michael was all too eager to please so that his grandpa would forget some of Michael's behavior over the last few days.

Just as they stepped up onto the sidewalk an explosion, three blocks down, rumbled the ground under their feet. Michael looked up he saw a big black cloud shoot out at a forty-five degree angle that was filled with metal, concrete, glass and other debris. Several big columns of fire shot up all around the debris and over the road.

Michael immediately reached out to steady Grandpa Dale who nearly stumbled right over when the blast hit. Michael, however, kept his head turned toward the blast area.

Suddenly, from the cloud of debris he saw a bulky shadow moving around. The sound of screeching metal then cut through the air. Suddenly, a car came rolling down the middle of the street, flipping end for end as it approached. It landed a block away from Michael and Grandpa Dale, then rolled to a halt less than thirty yards from where they stood.

"Come on, Grandpa. We have to get out of here," Michael said, trying to lead his grandfather toward the entrance of the building.

Peopled were screaming and running frantically all over the sidewalk. Many were also cutting across the road. Cars were stopping suddenly and even swerving sharply and minor collisions could be heard all along the roadway. Michael had his left arm wrapped around Grandpa Dale's waist and his right hand clasped around his arm. Grandpa Dale's cane had fallen back by the curb. They had to go slowly as people ran for cover, stopping suddenly several times as people cut directly in front of them.

The sounds of crunching metal and crumbling brick could be heard back at the blast zone. Michael kept turning toward the debris cloud trying to gauge the situation as best he could. He was also trying to ensure the safety of his blind grandfather. At last Michael reached the building entrance. Michael took his right arm away from Grandpa Dale to reach up for the door. Then he felt a tug on his left arm, and then suddenly nothing. When he looked back he saw that Grandpa Dale had stumbled and had fallen to all fours.

"Grandpa!" Michael yelled out.

Michael let go of the door and stepped back to Grandpa Dale. He took a quick glance over his shoulder and saw a shadowy figure grow large and then emerge from the cloud. He only got a quick look, but from what he saw, the source of all this chaos was a man. He seemed shorter than he expected, but very stalky. Thick armor coated much of his body. Then he was gone and another crash echoed up the street as the figure crashed through the wall of an adjacent building. Michael quickly grabbed Grandpa Dale under the arms and helped him back to his feet. He saw that Grandpa Dale was panting heavily and going pale. A middle aged man emerged from the building and came to their side and helped Michael carry Grandpa Dale through the front entrance. Once they were inside, another man, wearing a long white doctor's coat, came over to them.

"How are you feeling, sir?" the doctor asked, putting his index and middle fingers to Grandpa Dale's throat.

"Just a little shook up. I think I just need to sit for a moment," Grandpa Dale replied.

Michael and the middle aged man led him over to a nearby bench in the lobby. The doctor followed them and continued to look over Grandpa Dale, checking all of his vital signs. Michael glanced around and heard the worried buzz that was washing over the people sequestered there. The lobby was filling up quickly. Most people were either on the phone or trying to glance out the glass front doors. No one left the building and ventured into the street. The fragments of conversation that he was able to pick up were that everyone was assuming the city was under attack again. The sound of sirens could be heard closing in on the area. Another crash rumbled from down the street and shook the lobby beneath Michael's feet.

Michael felt that old familiar urge to rush off and transform into Titan straight away. He could almost feel the power pulse through his body as the lightning would envelope him already. He also knew that he couldn't just leave Grandpa Dale. He couldn't get Carly or anyone else to come to him this time either. The doctor had moved on to check other people in the lobby who were either hurt or having a hard time as well. Michael forced the urge to transform back, and came over and knelt by his grandfather.

"Grandpa, are you starting to feel any better?" he asked.

Grandpa Dale was taking long deep breaths with his head pointed down and his hands resting firmly on the bench at his sides.

"Well, the old ticker seems to be slowing down," Grandpa Dale replied between breaths, his hand pressed to his chest.

"I think I'm just gonna go around and see if I can find out what's happening, okay?" said Michael.

Grandpa Dale nodded slowly.

Michael rested his right hand on his grandfather's lap, looking at him worriedly. Grandpa Dale's own hand came and went over Michael's and rubbed it soothingly. Michael found it somewhat funny that even in his current condition his grandfather was worrying about him and not himself. Suddenly his hand seemed to stop over his index finger, the finger which held the magic ring. His hand ran back across it several times. Michael noticed his face suddenly pull tight, perplexed. Michael realized that Grandpa Dale had never felt his ring there before, therefore he had no way of knowing about it unless Michael told him, which he hadn't. Michael quickly withdrew his hand.

"Sure, why don't you see if you can find out what's going on," Grandpa Dale said, his hand on his lap, fingers moving like the ring was still beneath them.

"Okay, I'll be back as soon as I can," Michael said. He glanced out the front windows and saw thick black smoke billowing up the street. Then he quickly added, "Don't worry while I'm gone through."

"Just be careful, Michael," Grandpa Dale said quietly.

Michael stood and took one more long look at his grandfather. He had no idea what he was about to jump into, but he knew that if something happened to Grandpa Dale while he was gone he would never forgive himself.

Michael turned and began to walk to the front doors. More and more people were spilling into the lobby from the upper floor of the building. He quickly pulled out his cell and began to call Carly. He paused just in front of the main doors as it rang. On the third ring she picked up.

"Hello," Carly said.

"Carly, I need your help right away. Something big is going on down here and I have to get to it."

"Oh no, you're there! I was just watching some if it on TV. I was just hoping you both were nowhere near it," said Carly.

"It's happening just down the street. We're inside the clinic building right now, in the lobby. Grandpa Dale started having chest pains again. I can't leave him alone but I can't just let this happen either. This could be my chance to get to Dr. Melodian."

"Oh, I don't know how I could get there now. I couldn't even get a cab or a bus without a pass," Carly said.

"I'm sorry I just don't know who else I could ask."

"What about Vince?" Carly asked hesitantly.

Michael was stunned to silence. She was right, the only other person whose responsibility it would be was definitely Vince. He would also qualify to travel for family emergency. All he could think about then was what Grandpa Dale had said that morning about them both as brothers.

"Okay, I'll try and get a hold of him," Michael said.

As soon as he hung up with Carly, he scrolled through his contacts and went down to Vince's name. It was a number he had not used in some time, and had actually hardly ever used at all. He hit the name but didn't call instead deciding to text his brother.

> VINCE, WE ARE AT THE CLINIC.
> THERE IS AN ATTACK JUST DOWN THE STREET.
> GRANDPA HAVING SEVERE CHEST PAINS AGAIN.
> I NEED YOU HERE NOW.

Michael hit send, and then waited patiently for a response. Every second felt like hours and then about thirty seconds later a response came.

> I DON'T CARE WHAT YOU NEED IT WAS YOUR RESPONSIBILITY.

Michael could feel his anger boil over and was glad he had decided not to call. It only could have made things worse for Grandpa Dale if Michael started shouting at his brother in the crowded lobby. Michael began to type again.

IT'S NOT ABOUT ME AND IT'S NOT ABOUT YOU.
DO THIS FOR GRANDPA. YOU OWE HIM THAT MUCH AT LEAST.

Michael hit send and then waited for a response once again. This time it came much quicker.

FINE! I'LL COME WHEN I CAN.

With a weird sense of hesitant relief, Michael closed his phone and slipped it back into his pocket. He looked out of the windows, and saw that the thick smoke had moved so far up the street that he could barely see the other side of the road. He took a deep breath, opened the door and slid out. No one even seemed to notice as he went. He saw shadows moving farther down the road where the commotion had first started. Michael could hear the loud clang of debris falling nearby, but could not quite make out what was falling next to him. He quickly ran to where the smoke was the thickest and stopped abruptly. He held out his hand that held the magic ring and said the words aloud.

"Exaudio Fortis!"

No one was able to see the blast of blue lightning that crashed into Michael with the thick black smoke shrouding him. It looked like nothing more than part of the chaos that was taking over that part of the city.

Titan took out his staff, held it overhead, and began to spin it around as fast as he could. Much of the smoke was suddenly sucked into a giant funnel upwards. As the smoke cleared Titan saw that the fires had come from a row of cars that had been parked on the side of the street. He could make out about five scorched cars. He glanced up, the smoke continued to move upward and saw that the military helicopter was now hovering overhead. Then Titan looked down the street and saw the cause of all this havoc.

In the middle of the street about a half a block away, a very large man stood wearing numerous pieces of body armor. He was of average height, but very broad shouldered and wide bodied. He wore a metal helmet that covered the top of his head and was indented. He wore, what Titan could only think of as, some kind of futuristic football pads on his shoulders. They were large, metal, and covered the entire area around his shoulders. He also had smaller pieces around parts of his arms and legs. Giant armored gloves covered his club-like hands. Just like Sonic, he had what looked like some grenades strapped to his belt, which suddenly explained the burnt cars that lined the street behind him.

"Well, well, well, you must be Titan!" said the man.

Titan said nothing. He simply turned and faced the man head on. His staff was firmly gripped and ready to strike as his body tensed preparing for the inevitable battle that was sure to ensue.

"When the boss sent the others they were only to do as much damage to the city as possible. When he sent me, he told me to focus on you," the man said. With each word he took another step closer. "Once you're gone we all get to come out and play."

"Well, play time might just be over," Titan said.

"Oh we'll see," said the man.

"So, what clever nickname did Dr. Melodian give you?"

"Hammerhead, you can call me Hammerhead," Hammerhead replied with a devilish grin.

"Well, I can ask you some questions about your boss now, but I'm assuming you won't want to tell me anything, is that right?" Titan asked.

Hammerhead shook his head slowly, continuing toward Titan. His massive hands closed and opened from tight fists. Then suddenly Hammerhead dropped low and charged at Titan like a rampaging rhino. Using his staff, Titan was able to vault over him easily and land in a crouching position while Hammerhead charged past with a loud roar. There was a deafening crash as Hammerhead ploughed through a brick wall and into a clothing store. Titan turned to see where he was, but all he saw was a big pile of bricks and metal and a big black space. Suddenly, Hammerhead stepped through the hole, brushing off dust and debris from his armored shoulders.

"Oh, that's cute. You think you're pretty fast, huh?" Hammerhead said, climbing over the pile of crushed bricks toward Titan.

"Looks like I'm a whole lot faster than you are," Titan replied.

Titan began to sidestep to his right and was trying to move farther down the street away from the clinic building where Grandpa Dale currently was. He was already over a half a block away.

"Well, I think I have something that may slow you down some," Hammerhead said, with another grin.

Hammerhead reached down and pulled one of the grenades from his belt. He popped the pin and lobbed it at Titan. As it came at him in the middle of the street he prepared to dodge the blast when it suddenly went off about six feet from him. It didn't explode with the usual bang, however. It blew into a giant fiery blast that enveloped him. It blocked his view from everything else around him. He never did see Hammerhead coming before he collided with him and found himself trampled.

As Hammerhead's helmet hit Titan squarely in the chest, Titan thought at first he had been shot with a cannon. The collision drove Titan to the ground with tremendous force. Hammerhead barely even slowed, however, as he ploughed over him like a rag doll then rammed into a parked bus that nearly bent in two when he smashed into it dead center.

"What's the matter? Weren't fast enough for that one?" Hammerhead said with a chuckle, peeling himself off the bus.

This opponent is much stronger than he appears.

"Yeah, thanks for that, but I already kinda figured that one out on my own," Titan said sarcastically, staggering to his feet.

As the two of them were about to square off, there was suddenly a loud rumble sending small tremors rolling right to their feet. As Titan looked all around he saw that four tanks had moved from all intersecting streets, and with the helicopter overhead all points of exit were now cut off. He looked back to Hammerhead who seemed largely unfazed and focused entirely on Titan.

"So, what's your plan for them then?" Titan asked gesturing to the tanks. "You can't beat us all you know."

"Oh, you're about to see exactly what I can do," Hammerhead said.

Hammerhead suddenly charged at Titan. Titan was easily able to leap away, but Hammerhead kept going. He charged right passed Titan and through a small sedan. It blew into metallic splinters all over the road and sidewalk on impact. Hammerhead kept on going through. Titan was wondering if he was also blind, as he went straight at a brick wall without even slowing. The wall broke apart just as easily as before, but Hammerhead did not reappear. Titan could still hear him crashing through the dark deserted building destroying anything in his path.

Titan quickly moved toward the gaping hole in the side of the building. The crashing sound of Hammerhead's wake was growing more distant until suddenly with one final crash he could see daylight from the far side of the building. He could just make out the shape of Hammerhead on the other side as he stepped onto the street and turned right. Titan glanced up over his shoulder and saw the military helicopter bank away from the street toward where Hammerhead now was. The tanks also began to pull away and move in his direction.

"This isn't good," Titan exclaimed.

No, it certainly is not. You must locate Hammerhead at once.

"Well, I hate to say it, but I think the military can handle him just fine now. Maybe I can just get back to my grandpa."

Titan, you know your responsibility. Who knows the extent of damage Hammerhead can do before he is brought down by them. It is you that has the power to do it.

Titan stood still a moment staring at the giant hole in the brick wall in front of him, thinking. Then he turned and looked back down the block toward the building where he had left Grandpa Dale. He slumped his shoulders and hung his head momentarily. Then he pulled out his staff, looked up and leaped to the top of the building in front of him.

From the rooftop, he scanned the city skyline and spotted the military helicopter a couple of blocks over, hovering.

"Looks like we have our guy right over there. At least he'll be easier to follow than Hawk," Titan said, as he was already coiling his legs preparing to leap.

Remember, Titan, you now know something of this opponent and know what he is capable of and can even use some of his strengths against him. Also, despite what these authorities may be thinking about you, they are still your allies. Use them against this foe if possible. This may even be able to help you in your current standing with the authorities here.

"Gotcha, I'll do whatever I can, but most importantly I want information about Dr. Melodian," Titan said, as he soared through the air and landed deftly on a rooftop adjacent to the helicopter.

Agreed! We need to get to him above all else to end this madness.

Titan looked directly below. He saw Hammerhead charging down the center of King St. Police cruisers with lights flashing dotted the corridor. Hammerhead would occasionally veer to the right or left plowing into parked vehicles nearly shredding smaller cars in two and taking two bigger vehicles and capsizing them onto the sidewalk. The police cruisers backed off the street leaving King St, open and preparing themselves to hold Hammerhead there. From Titan's view it looked as though he were thoroughly enjoying his rampage down one of Delta City's busiest thoroughfares.

Then, just as Hammerhead passed the 12th Ave intersection, one of the tanks lumbered into view directly behind him, seemingly unnoticed. Titan watched with rapt attention while the tank lifted its massive cannon, and with a deafening blast, fired a shot toward the havoc of Hammerhead. He hardly seemed to notice, however, as the shot rang over his head and crashed into the street in front of him tearing a massive hole into the asphalt. He simply continued to tear through a jeep abandoned in the middle of the street.

Before the tank's cannon could reposition to fire another round, Titan leaped from his rooftop perch and angled himself straight at Hammerhead. He crashed right into his back driving him face first into the street. They rolled to a stop about ten yards ahead. Titan quickly jumped to his feet with his staff ready to battle. Hammerhead was slow to rise and when he did his face was bloodied and his body armor scraped up badly. Otherwise he seemed simply angry and ready to engage Titan.

"You're gonna pay for that one!" Hammerhead roared at Titan.

He dropped low and charged, moving at Titan like a small truck. Titan waited until the last possible moment and then used his staff to vault over him with ease. Titan landed on the top of a semi-trailer looking down at Hammerhead.

"I'm sorry, how was I going to pay again?" Titan mocked from up high.

Titan noticed from his peripheral vision that the adjoining streets were quickly blocking up with military vehicles. After seeing the tank fire at Hammerhead, Titan knew they were going to take no chance of him getting loose again.

"Oh, you'll pay alright. First I'm gonna get my hands on you and then I'll make you watch as I tear this city apart with the entire boss' army behind me," Hammerhead seethed.

Hammerhead charged from thirty yards out. Titan crouched and readied his stance. He noticed one of the tanks again roll right into the middle of the street behind Hammerhead. Hammerhead was focused only on Titan. The end of Titan's staff buzzed with brilliant blue light as he leaped from the trailer top straight at him. He fired a massive lightning blast as his feet left the edge. The blast connected with Hammerhead's metal helmet and he seemed to freeze mid-stride while caught in the current. Before the blast had faded, Titan once again collided with the lumbering hulk with both fists planted firmly into his chest.

Titan rolled to a stop and looked over his shoulder at Hammerhead. He lay in a heap in the middle of the street, face down, smoke emanating from his body. Titan moved in quickly as he began to stir. He sheathed his staff and grabbed hold of Hammerhead by the shoulders and spun him around. He ripped the battered helmet from his head and quickly went to work doing the same to the rest of Hammerhead's armor. He then pulled out his staff once again and aimed its end to Hammerhead's throat.

"Now, I have some questions I'd like to ask you about Dr. Melodian," Titan said.

I think you'd best take notice of your surroundings, Titan!

At Azure's words, Titan glanced up to see a terrifying sight. Armed military personnel had surrounded the two of them with weapons aimed. Titan froze instantly. Only his eyes darted all around, surveying the extent of the situation. He had no idea how they could have moved in so fast without him noticing, even if he had been focused on Hammerhead. Suddenly, a man stepped forward. It was the same man he had noticed from his earlier altercations with Sonic and with Hawk. He was older and had a big bushy gray moustache.

"I'm gonna have to ask you to step down, son," General Stevenson asked Titan.

The general stood stone-faced staring straight at Titan. His men seemed frozen awaiting the orders to either fire or stand down themselves. Titan stood in place part out of fear and partly out of confusion. He let his body relax and loosen. At last he stood upright and sheathed his staff once again.

"I just need to get some information from him. I need to get to Dr. Melodian," Titan said, his eyes darting upward, searching for an escape route.

The General's eyes suddenly went wide in what seemed a rare show of emotion.

"How do you know about him?" General Stevenson asked.

"I have my sources."

"Well, the good doctor is our problem and we intend to take care of it," General Stevenson said, as he began to pace around Titan. "We do appreciate you taking out this guy for us, but we can take it from here. Understand?"

"You guys couldn't handle Hammerhead, what makes you think that you can go after Melodian without my help. In fact, I also seem to remember you and your little team there having problems stopping Sonic and Hawk too," said Titan.

The general suddenly stopped in his tracks and glared at Titan. Titan tensed instantly his hands quickly forming into fists and the muscles in his legs tightening, readying for action.

"Son, er Titan is it? You were in our way as much as you helped us on both those other occasions. The only reason we have let you continue in the manner you have is that we have no orders regarding you, whether to eliminate you as a threat or take you in for interrogation. Unless, of course, you are interfere with my orders. I will admit to you though, the mayor was trying to make a hard case that we take you in with us along with Melodian. The point here, however, is that Dr. Karl Melodian is a military problem and the military intends to take care of it."

"Well, Delta City is under my protection so now he's my problem, too. So, what are you going to do if I won't leave?" challenged Titan.

General Stevenson didn't even flinch as Titan spoke. Once he was done the general simply stood there facing Titan emotionless.

"Look, maybe we can compromise a little here. It's your guy in my city, right? Why don't we work together here and bring him in?" Titan asked.

General Stevenson's eyes grew to slits as he took careful, slow steps toward Titan. Then his arms clasped together at his back indicating that he would wait to hear what Titan proposed.

"Well, I don't like the idea of the military accepting aid like this, but I also don't like the idea of sending my men up against you either. So, just how do you propose we work together?" asked General Stevenson.

"It's simple, really. We find out where the mad doctor is hiding by asking bozo here," Titan said, gesturing toward Hammerhead. "Then, I go in and either capture him myself or flush him out to you and your men. I have strong reason to believe that he's in an underground lair."

General Stevenson cracked a smile at Titan. Then he tilted his head from side to side as he seemed to weigh his proposal. Titan stood perfectly still in front of the general waiting for his response. He was trying his best to look nowhere as nervous as he actually was. He could feel the sweat pouring down his forehead and back. He let his eyes drift up and all around. Now there were police snipers that had crept to the rooftops of surrounding buildings. What appeared to be members of the media had also managed to position themselves at high windows with a bird's eye view of the events.

"If you allow my men to mike you and attach a homing beacon, we can keep tabs on your whereabouts when you go down there, you have a deal. Otherwise I'm afraid I'll still have to insist that you step aside, and I do mean remove you by force if necessary."

"Fine, whatever makes you happy," Titan responded.

Titan, I am not sure this is a good idea. The authorities here have not been overly understanding or supportive of your endeavors to date.

"It's cool, Azure," Titan whispered, while trying to turn away from the general, who was busy gesturing to his men. He figured being caught talking to a disembodied spirit guide would not be a good way to show he was to be trusted. "Like you said, we have to find a way to prove to people that we're one of the good guys."

You speak true. I simply ask you to be cautious.

Titan did not answer. He simply turned back to the general.

"Well, I suppose we have to get some information from him then," General Stevenson said, pointing again to Hammerhead.

"Don't worry, I think I have this one too," Titan said with a coy grin.

He turned back to Hammerhead who had been laying there helpless at Titan's feet the entire time. His broken armor littered the ground all around him. Titan pulled out his staff and held the jeweled end directly in front of his face. Blue sparks began to erupt and sizzle from it.

"So, tell me, just where can I find your boss?

CHAPTER 11: Passage of Doom

"You don't have the guts to take on the doc, he has the guts to take you guys on though, don't worry about that one. You'll see soon enough anyway," Hammerhead said, as he tried to scramble away on his back.

"What, do you really think if you talk that we'll just toss you back to him?" Titan said, blue electrical current still sizzled and sparked from the end of his staff.

"You don't even know what you're up against. I've seen what he has. I know what he can do. I don't even know if the likes of you can stop him," Hammerhead said to Titan. The cocky confidence had left. His face now showed nothing but fear when speaking of Dr. Melodian.

"You have no idea what I'm capable of, pal," Titan shot right back.

Hammerhead then gazed around at the strong military presence around him. His eyes darted about like a frightened cornered animal. Titan's staff suddenly went silent as he brought it back upright at his side.

"Alright, I'll point you in the right direction, but I'm going nowhere near him. I'll stay with your buddies here," Hammerhead said, gesturing General Stevenson and his men behind Titan.

"That's all I need."

Hammerhead then slowly raised himself first to a sitting position and then he slowly got to his feet and stood facing Titan. He then extended his right hand toward Titan. Titan looked back at the general, but Stevenson was once again stone-faced and emotionless. Titan saw nothing that could possibly go wrong with a simple handshake, especially if it made him more comfortable in co-operating, so he extended his hand. Hammerhead grasped Titan's hand. He squeezed it tight and pulled him close before whispering to him.

"I never wanted to do any of this. The doc just has a way of being pretty persuasive," Hammerhead said in a low voice. "I have a wife. He has her. He made me do this, so I had to or he said he would kill her. He's done the same to some of the others. Just promise me that you can protect her from him," Hammerhead pleaded.

"I promise you that I'll do whatever I can to protect her and all of the others too," Titan said, as he released his hand from Hammerhead's.

There were snipers and tanks still aimed at him, but Hammerhead's body seemed to relax and settle with Titan's promise. He took a deep breath and looked back behind General Stevenson as though searching for something.

"Okay, he's underground," Hammerhead said in a quiet voice.

"Impossible," General Stevenson blurted. "We've searched the entire city, including the subway system and sewers."

"No, he's not on any of your grids or systems. I mean he's underground, deep underground," Hammerhead said. He then pointed back at the giant hole made by the tank earlier. "You can enter through the sewers, but you'll have to keep going down. It's pretty easy to find. Hawk and Sonic both found their way back easy enough, and they're idiots."

"Perez, bring me the city maps, all of them," General Stevenson said, as he brought a walkie-talkie from his hip to his mouth.

Minutes later numerous maps were laid out over the hood of a nearby military jeep. The one that was the current focal point showed the layout and grid of the city's underground sewer. General Stevenson and two of his men hovered over one side of the map as they watched closely while Hammerhead pointed to several key areas. Titan remained closest to Hammerhead, ready to act swiftly if needed, as he was still not entirely trustworthy.

"If you follow this line right here it'll take you to the passage of doom."

"The passage of doom? You've got to be kidding me; this guy actually has something called the passage of doom," Titan remarked.

"He called it that because he lined the entire thing with cameras and traps. If one of us enters we can get access, but if he sees any intruders he can remotely spring any of the traps lining the passageway to his main headquarters," Hammerhead answered.

"What kind of traps are we talking about here?" General Stevenson asked, never taking his eyes from the map.

"I don't really know. We just knew if we brought back intruders that he could kill us without even entering the passageway himself."

"Well, this just keeps getting better and better," Titan chimed in.

"I don't know what else I can tell you, sorry," Hammerhead said.

"Okay, here goes nothing then," Titan said, turning toward the massive hole in the street that the tank had caused earlier.

"Not so fast," General Stevenson said, finally turning away from the map. "Let me have my men give you that two-way mike and GPS. If we can keep tabs on you and we can communicate with you down there, then we can always send backup if you do find yourself in a bind."

"Um…yeah, I don't think I like the sound of that," Titan responded.

"I need to know what goes on down there. I can also guide you with the map from up here," General Stevenson said.

Titan, I believe that this is a worthy solution. They cannot harm or control you in any way with any of their technology. You must also trust them if you want them to trust you.

"Fine, let's do this then," Titan said.

General Stevenson had one of his men equip Titan for his journey to Dr. Melodian. A short thin soldier approached Titan and clipped a small box onto his belt on his left side. He then brought out an ear piece for the two-way communication link. Titan's mask, however, was covering both of his ears. Titan could sense the soldier gauging the mask and the earpiece in his hand, and his reluctance to lift the mask at all to attach the ear piece.

"Here, I can handle it, thanks," Titan said, as he snatched the ear piece from the soldier's hand.

"If he's right," General Stevenson said, referring to Hammerhead, "then Dr. Melodian's location is under the downtown of the city. A direct strike from us is basically out of the question. In a pinch we can flood the area with men and attack the good doctor. I don't really like that either, though. It leaves my men stuck fighting in this tight little tube essentially with little room to move around or escape. So, basically we really need you to get in there and take him down fast and bring him back to us, got it?"

"I think I can handle it," Titan said, finishing attaching the ear piece under his mask. A small arm poked out from under the mask and stopped at his right cheek.

Titan walked over to the massive hole in the street. As he stood at the edge and peered in, he could see the water from the city sewer flow below street level. He took one last look at the military that formed a tight perimeter around the street and the police officers that lined many of the rooftops. As if on cue the helicopter made a pass overhead.

"Well, let's get to it then," Titan said. He then leaped down to the sewer below.

Titan made his way down the middle of the sewer stream and followed the running water as it moved further into the city. He passed from the crater in the street overhead, and the sewer became enclosed again. Titan looked up and found the pipe that Hammerhead had mentioned and began to follow it.

"Titan, you find the line you needed?" General Stevenson asked through the earpiece.

"Yeah, I have it," Titan answered.

"Okay, in about a hundred yards you should be coming to a big opening with a bunch of tunnels in front of you. Let me know once you get there." General Stevenson said.

Titan plodded on through the murky sewer water. Smaller tunnels opened and went in various directions, but he continued to follow the pipeline as outlined by Hammerhead. Then, he came to a massive opening. There was a giant area that opened to about fifty feet across in a rounded room. At the opposite end from Titan there were three passageways.

"Okay, I'm here and I see the tunnels right up ahead. Which one do I take?" Titan asked into his microphone.

Titan could hear some muffled voices on the other end of his earpiece before he got a response.

"You want the tunnel on the far left. It should be more dimly lit than the other two. Now, be careful as you approach the tunnel. Once you reach the entrance you could be facing any type, or any number of traps. We've all seen what Melodian is capable of, so you can guarantee that once we start to penetrate his hideout, he will start to pull out all the aces he's been hiding up his sleeve," General Stevenson said.

"Got it," Titan responded, as he reached the entryway of the left tunnel.

"Right now we have your location. Hopefully, as you go deeper, the GPS signal holds. If it doesn't, the mike should."

"Sounds good, General. I'm at the tunnel and about to go in. I'll keep you posted on what I see."

Titan, do not take this lightly. We have no way of knowing what awaits you through this passageway. Remain ready and cautious.

Titan didn't respond for fear that General Stevenson would hear him. He simply entered the tunnel. Instantly, he heard a loud click and hum. There was the briefest moment where he felt the hairs on his arm and the back of his neck stand up. Then, suddenly, massive jolts of electricity shot out from the doorframe and began to electrocute him.

Titan was frozen in a strong current of electric shock for ten seconds. When it stopped, he dropped to his knees clutching his side with both hands. He looked around to see smoke rising from his own body. He began to get to his feet carefully when he heard the click and hum begin again. He quickly ducked and rolled forward into the tunnel. Bright yellow electrical current suddenly shot out and filled the entry.

"I think he's watching the entrance, General," Titan said into his mike.

There was no response from the earpiece. Titan tapped the earpiece and got nothing. He then pulled off the GPS from his belt. The screen had gone entirely black. He dropped the GPS to the ground and let the water swallow it up.

"Well, that's fried," Titan said, dropping the earpiece to the same fate as the GPS.

Our enemy seems ready for our arrival. You will have to move forward with extreme caution. The path from here forward will likely only get more treacherous.

"Yeah, I hear ya there."

Titan then pulled out his staff, leveled it at the archway and fired a lightning blast at it. The blast reverberated through the tunnel. Brick and metal exploded from the archway scattering every which way. Titan stood firm, as fragments bounced off his chest and arms. Once the dust cleared an array of electrical components were left exposed from behind where the brick had been. Small sparks were still being spat out of the ends of some wires and metal pipe.

Why did you feel that to be necessary?

"Um, I just thought, why leave it active like that? Now that we've lost communication to General Stevenson they're likely to send a team down soon to come after Melodian themselves," Titan answered.

Very well, that is excellent planning ahead for your allies.

Titan didn't respond, but he was unable to repress a grin from creeping across his face. He continued down the watery path ahead. He had no way of knowing what awaited him next, he could only be sure that something would be. He moved with his back and shoulders hunched ready for the next attack. Both hands remained firmly gripped on his staff.

As Titan moved on, the dull grey brick that lined the tunnel walls suddenly gave way to solid metal panels. The water that ran down the middle of the tunnel had faded to practically nothing. Before the walls changed, every so often the walls displayed directional signs indicating certain water lines or other information city workers would need. These seemed to stop too.

Titan could see nowhere for a trap to be hidden as the entire tunnel was now nothing more than one tight metal tube. Even the floor was now lined with the same metal tiles that lined the walls. He was even scanning the ceiling above for a possible trap, but he could see none.

"I don't know, things look pretty clear as far as I…"

Before Titan could even finish his thought, a deafening rumble cut through the air. Suddenly, Titan caught a glimpse of shining metal to his left that wasn't there a moment before. He moved slightly to his right, and just as he did a giant metal blade came spinning out of the wall. The blade was quite thin and at least four feet wide with long jagged edges. It had shot out from between the cracks of the paneling. Then, he felt the ground tremble, and several pointy edges poked out from between his feet. Titan dove forward and rolled to a quick stop. Suddenly the loud rumble increased and blades began to shoot out from other cracks all along the floor and walls, with one even protruding from the ceiling.

Titan could feel his senses heightened and on edge. He deftly leaped from every blade as it shot out toward him. He became vaguely aware that, as each blade popped out it caused him to move deeper within the tunnel, like he were being herded like cattle. One blade that shot out from his right side caught him off guard and slashed open the side of his uniform gashing him in the process. Titan grabbed at his side and plunged forward where he promptly tripped and nearly fell on a blade that had popped out from the ground. He was able to spin and regain some footing.

Titan glanced up ahead and could see that the lighting dimmed and the metal paneling seemed to fade back to brick. The tunnel was tight and left little room for him to use his powers effectively, but he was able to push off of one foot into a leap that shot him straight through the middle of the tunnel. He landed with a hard splash as water had also once again begun to wash in from drains that lined the upper part of the wall. As Titan tried to catch his breath he sat in waist deep water.

"So, that's where he hid the traps," Titan exclaimed breathlessly.

You must not rest now, Titan. You must keep going.

"Okay, okay I'm going."

Titan pivoted to get his feet back under him so he could stand. As he bent forward with his face only inches from the murky water, he suddenly saw two glowing blue orbs just beneath the surface. Titan froze and his eyes narrowed to slits as he tried to make out what was floating beneath him. The blue orbs quickly enlarged as they drew nearer to the surface. Titan suddenly leaned back so far that he found himself once again sitting in waist deep water. Once he plopped back into the water he glanced around and saw three other sets of blue lights hovering around him. He looked back as the first set of blue lights broke the surface and he was able to see what they were.

The blue orbs were the eyes of a small robotic creature that had the shape of a spider. It had an oval body about two and half feet long like a big metal football. It sat on six spindly metal legs. On its back, a hole opened and a small arm came out and curled around like a scorpion tail so the tip of it faced Titan. He quickly looked around at the other three and saw that they all looked the same and a similar contraption was emerging from their backs as well. On one was a small blade. On another he made out small rockets attached to it. The one to his left had a small machine gun aimed at him. He came back to the one right in front of him and saw that a metal tail tip was aimed at him. Then, the tip glowed fiercely red.

"Uh oh, this won't be good," Titan groaned.

Titan lunged to the right just as the spiderbot's red tail flashed a laser beam that just sailed over his head and crashed into the sewer wall in a cloud of concrete and dust. He quickly shot his right leg out and connected with the little robot sending it flying backwards and into the opposite wall where it crashed.

Before he knew it the sound of the whirring blade on the one to his right was in his ear. Titan rolled just as the blade came slashing down for him. He was able to get his knees back under him and in a position to get to his feet. His right foot touched ground and he reached out and grabbed the Spiderbot's tail at the base and lifted it into the air. The Spiderbot with the machine gun started firing, leaving a trail of bullet holes along the wall that seemed to be chasing Titan. He spun and launched the captured bladed Spiderbot at it. The two collided in a tiny explosion.

The bot with the rockets began running at him with alarming speed. Once it was halfway, it began to fire its rockets. Three little rockets shot off the tail and sailed toward him. They left little vapor trails in the tunnel as they went. Titan batted the first one away with his staff and it sailed a few feet before exploding in midair. The other two were too fast for him and collided into his chest and stomach leaving charred black marks on his uniform. Titan dropped to one knee clutching his stomach. With one arm he swung his staff around and fired a lightning blast at the Spiderbot that incinerated it instantly.

Suddenly, he felt a sharp hot sting singe the back of his left shoulder. He dropped further forward just as he felt the heat of another laser blast go sailing past. He turned to see the first Spiderbot scamper over to him. It moved so fast that it was easily able to scale the wall and run alongside it while firing off laser blasts from its tail. Titan dodged them easily enough, but instead of moving away from it he went toward it with his staff extended. Two more blasts connected to the front of his shoulder and his right hip. Finally, Titan jabbed the end of his staff right through its back with a loud crack and sizzle.

"Well, looks like we can…" Titan began.

Roughly twenty yards ahead the sight of seven more sets of glowing blue eyes moving toward him from beneath the water stunned him to silence. They moved in a V pattern, like one big arrow pointed straight at Titan. He gripped his staff tightly with both hands and paused as though unsure whether to stand and fight or run. Suddenly, all seven broke the surface. Their tails protruded simultaneously and their tips flashed red. Titan turned and began to run.

Laser blasts sailed past him from all over. Some collided with the sides of the tunnel sending out bits of concrete that stung at Titan's face and arms. The splashing sound they made as they chased grew louder and louder. He aimed his staff behind him blindly and fired two blasts of his own trying not to break stride, spotting a turn up ahead and preparing to use it to lose them.

The tunnel curved slightly to the left. Titan took the corner with ease, and when he glanced over his shoulder he saw that some of the Spiderbots simply raced up along the wall. All of them continued to fire at him mercilessly. One shot caught the back of his thigh, Titan stumbled forward crashing to the ground in a big splash.

Two bots were on him instantly. One fired a shot that grazed off the top of his head. Titan was able to grab hold of them, one in each hand and slam them to the surface. Both were crushed. He looked over and saw that the rest were bearing down quickly. Up ahead he saw two passages. He quickly got back to his feet and headed for them. He could only hope that one lead to safety.

Titan fought through the pain he felt all over, and raced for the passage on the right. Just as he was about to go through it, several laser shots crashed into the archway destroying it. Titan was knocked aside with his arms up to shield his face. He then stepped into the passage on the left. His foot went through to the other side and found nothing but dark open air as he fell into pure blackness.

CHAPTER 12: Double Down

Titan landed face first in more water with a giant splash. He hit the concrete floor with a hard thud. His body ached all over. He slowly got up to his knees and looked around. The entire area was in complete darkness. He looked back up the shaft he had just fallen through and saw a big circle of light. Suddenly, the whole area flooded with bright light causing Titan to squint his eyes.

His eyes slowly started to adjust to the bright light. He saw that he was in a large circular room with a ceiling that ended some forty feet just above the doorway he had come through. There seemed to be two entrances to the room, on opposite sides of the wide room that ran about fifty yards across. He had dropped his staff during the fall. As it floated past, he bent over and scooped it up.

"This isn't good. I just keep getting pushed farther and farther down the rabbit hole," Titan said to Azure.

I am not sure I follow as I have seen no rabbits down here.

"It's just a reference to a ...ah never mind. I just mean this is going from bad to worse."

I do agree, however, that we are being pushed along where our enemy wants us to go.

"I guess I need to figure out which door I need to get to, and before some other trap comes..." Titan began, when a sudden blow struck him across the side of the face.

He fell backwards from the force of the unexpected blow. He found himself seated again with his knees poking from the water and his arms stretched back to keep him from getting fully submerged. A small orb with flashing red lights now bobbed in the water right in his lap. Titan recognized it instantly, and started to scramble away from it. He was trying to simultaneously kick it away and get to his feet, and as far away from it as he could. His errant kick flailed right past the orb, missing it completely. Knowing it was hopeless, Titan turned to get away just as it exploded with tremendous force.

Titan could feel the intense heat from the blast as he was sent flying forward. His staff was practically ripped from his hand in the blast. He was once again sent into the water face first. As he splashed into the water he was unable to avoid a large intake of breath and a big mouthful of water lodged in his throat. He popped up coughing and spitting out large amounts of dirty water. Panting and gasping for air, Titan got to all fours and began crawling forward with his eyes closed until he ran into a solid object. His hand ran over hard metal as he opened his eyes to find a metallic foot. He followed the foot up a familiar metal leg and saw the frantic face of Sonic staring back at him.

"You shouldn't be here," Sonic said, in a high cracking voice. His eyes were wide and he was breathing heavily.

"You're telling me," Titan responded, wearily.

Sonic dropped another orb in front of Titan and then vanished. Titan quickly pushed off with his arms and spun backwards just as the orb blew. This time he was able to avoid much of the blast. Water kicked up by the blast settled around him and waves slapped against the walls of the large room. He scrambled to his feet. He stood poised and ready with both hands up to fight, but Sonic was nowhere in sight.

He looked all over the room for his staff, and just as he spotted it at the far wall to his left, he felt a rush of wind from behind and a sudden blow to his lower back. Titan dropped down to one knee, his left hand clutching his back. He could see Sonic moving in a blur about the room in a trail of big waves that shot up in his wake. Titan spun around in all directions trying to get him in his sights to strike back. Before he could, however, he took another blow to the side of his face and was sent staggering back.

Before he could even regain any footing, he felt something whoosh past overhead. He looked up to see Hawk buzzing overhead in the tunnel. He was also armed with the explosive orbs and was dropping them from above.

"Let's see how you do now on our turf, tough guy," Hawk hollered, as he angled himself and flew toward the top of the room before rolling and rocketing himself back down toward Titan. He cackled gleefully while he dropped.

Titan tried his best to get his bearings and make his way across to where he last saw his staff. Sonic continued to kick up giant waves as ran past. Titan took his first stride forward, and Sonic caught him again, this time in the midsection, and Titan stumbled to his left. Still staggering, he glimpsed a blinking orb drop down at his side.

It exploded the second it hit the water's surface in a fiery blast. Titan was launched forward, all limbs flailing helplessly. All he was aware of was the sound of Hawk's jetpack trailing off and the waves being kicked up by Sonic as he crashed to the surface. It was at that moment he felt he was about to face his first real defeat as Titan. This was like no school sport he had ever played, however. Here one defeat could be all it took to ensure there would be no more chances. These thoughts were racing through his mind when he was using the last of his strength to pull himself back up. Just then, his staff floated under him as he crouched on all fours.

Seeing his staff seemed to rejuvenate Titan as he rushed to his feet, clutching it in his hands tightly. Sonic continued to race all around him. He could hear Hawk once again dive bomb from above. He raised his staff and turned it upside down. He knew that it was only mere moments before one of them struck again, but he had to wait to ensure getting them both. Then, just as Hawk lowered to the height of the waves kicked up by Sonic, Titan rammed his staff into the water and fired a massive blast of lightning.

The entire room suddenly shone a brilliant blue. Visible electric current seemed to wrap itself around the waves as they rose in the air. Titan could hear the screams of Hawk and Sonic as current ripped through his own body. He dropped to his knees. The waves stopped and he could see Sonic crumpled in the corner by one of the entrances. Titan propped himself up with his arms, when he spotted that Hawk had crashed five feet away in a smoking heap.

Titan stood wearily and sheathed his staff. His uniform was in tatters and he was bruised and battered all over. On legs that seemed made of Jell-O, he walked over to Sonic. He bent over and rolled Sonic onto his back. The water sizzled as his back touched it. Sonic was breathing but still unconscious. Titan turned and made his way over to Hawk.

As he approached, Hawk began moaning and moving his arms and legs slightly. Titan pulled his staff out and poked him twice with the end, ready to fire again if needed. Hawk managed to turn and look up, only to see Titan take his staff and quickly stab a hole in each of his wings.

"Do I have your attention now?" Titan said through panting breaths.

"Go ahead do your worst," Hawk barked back, suddenly surging back to life before quickly slumping back to a pile on the ground.

"This isn't a discussion. You're going to show me where Melodian is."

"I'm not...wait, what do you mean show you?" Hawk asked, eyes suddenly popping wide.

Titan did not respond. He grabbed Hawk by both shoulders and lifted him to his feet. While propping him up with one hand he used the other to rip the metal wings from Hawk's back. As he tossed the wings to the ground he shoved him forward. Hawk took two clumsy steps before crashing to his knees.

"No, I can't!" Hawk pleaded.

Titan simply aimed his staff at Hawk's chest, and pointed forward with his other hand. Hawk walked over to one of the two exits in the room and stopped at its entrance and stared forward. Hawk began to walk ahead hesitantly, his head constantly spinning back and forth to the path ahead and Titan behind him. Hawk continued through the open dark tunnel right in front.

"If I do this are you going to protect me from him?" Hawk began pleading.

"Just keep going," Titan snapped back.

Hawk continued nervously for another twenty yards through the near perfect dark tunnel. No other traps or robots or enemies of any kind popped out at them in this time. At last they reached a solid wall at the end of the path.

"This is it," Hawk said, exasperated, his head slumped forward against the hard wall surface.

"This, are you sure?" Titan asked.

Just then the wall flew upwards and a blinding white light filled the tunnel. A shot of something rang out and collided with Hawk's chest. He flew backwards landing in a heap on his back. Titan stood in shock and watched as Hawk rolled his side, unconscious. Titan stood watching in shock. He found himself give a sigh of relief as he saw Hawk's body rise and fall with slow steady breaths.

Three long thin cables suddenly shot out of the opening and wrapped themselves around Titan. He dropped to the ground as the cables bound his legs together, and another bound his arms and staff to his body, while a third wrapped around his neck and head.

"Welcome, Titan. I am glad you've finally made it. I would have hated it had you not been here to witness the destruction of your city," a calm mellow voice came from inside the room.

Thee cables squeezed tighter and tighter until Titan dropped to the ground helpless, and began to pull him into the opening.

CHAPTER 13: Dr. Melodian

"I had anticipated you becoming much more of a problem in my business here," Dr. Melodian said, as the cables continued to drag Titan into the bright room.

Titan's eyes adjusted to the light. He saw that he was a on a hard tiled floor and that the walls were also tiled. Large domed fluorescent lights hung overhead. There room was a large open squared space with large banks of computers and monitors all around the perimeter. There also seemed what appeared to be a small computer console in the middle of the room, where Dr. Melodian sat. The computer was silver and round and seemed to have numerous buttons and levers that faced him. At the bottom of the console facing Titan was a small opening where the cables that bound him were pulling him closer to Dr. Melodian.

Dr. Melodian himself looked rather professional and calm, as he sat at the console pressing buttons, reeling Titan in. He wore a neatly pressed white lab coat buttoned to the neck. He had black rubber gloves over his hands. His hair was neatly combed and he had a pair of black rimmed glasses that rested on his nose. In Titan`s opinion, Dr. Melodian looked quite the opposite of how he thought a mad scientist should look.

"You have barely tested the maximum potential of my restraints," Dr. Melodian continued. "I haven't even had to use the electric shock mechanism. Oh, but why not? I did go to all the trouble of installing it."

Suddenly, electric current surged through the cables that bound Titan. His body tensed and contorted from the shock as much as was possible against the restraints. The shock then subsided for the briefest moment letting his body relax before it surged back through his body again. He had no time to even try to resist between electric shocks. He felt utterly helpless against it.

"You have proven a great disappointment. Tell me, before you came down here, did General Stevenson really think he could take me so easily?"

Dr. Melodian asked.

The shocks subsided while Dr. Melodian waited for a response. Yet, Titan continued to be dragged slowly closer to the console which was now less than twenty feet away. Titan could tell from what he had just said that Dr. Melodian had clearly had closer tabs on the action above ground than any of them had previously thought. He was also clearly very confident that whatever plan he had could not be stopped by anyone.

"There is no point struggling. You are only wasting your energy," Dr. Melodian said flatly, his emotions never wavering.

"Why are you doing all of this?" Titan asked, relaxing his muscles.

"Because I have been wronged greatly, and will have my retribution. I will not be denied. They have taken so much from me; it is high time that I take something back," Dr. Melodian shot back, true anger showing through for the first time.

"But the people of Delta City weren't the ones who wronged you. Why are you taking this out on them? That's not fair," said Titan.

Dr. Melodian paused for a moment, stared at Titan being dragged across the floor toward him. He was nearly at the console now, less than twelve feet. Then, he smiled before responding to Titan. Long narrow teeth flashed like piano keys. Dr. Melodian moved his hand over the controls and suddenly another shockwave rolled up the cords that bound Titan. Titan's body convulsed violently, as much as the cords would allow.

"I did not bring them into this either. It was them, General Stevenson and his men. They are responsible for these events being brought about. I tried to reason with them, even after I was wronged, I tried. Then, I even tried to warn everyone, by virtually threatening them as to what I was capable. Yet I was laughed at. Well, are they laughing now?"

Another surge of electricity pulsed through the cables.

"I am not with them. I only want to keep the people of this city safe," declared Titan.

"The citizens will be safe once I exploit the weaknesses of this military and show them for what they are. Then, they will be liberated," Dr. Melodian explained.

Titan I fear this man is far beyond reasoning with. I think it best that you simply try to escape and find a way of stopping his machinations.

"You're not making any sense. What could they have possibly done to wrong you so much that you would be willing to put millions of innocent lives at stake," Titan said, figuring that he could at least buy some time.

"That's just it. I have already unknowingly killed untold millions. I once bought whatever cheap lines Stevenson and his peers sold to me."

Titan was now only a mere few feet from Dr. Melodian. As he approached, Titan began to rise in front of the console not of his own will or power. The cords binding him seemed to stiffen and shift him so that he was now virtually tied to an invisible chair in front of the console.

Dr. Melodian went on, "I worked for them since I was fresh out of university. I had always had a great love of science. I learned all that I could on my own from a very young age. I also learned that I had a certain knack for mechanical inventing. I was born without legs and at a very young age I saw what science and technology could do for me. I devoted my entire life to two things: science, and using it to enrich the lives of others. I was ready to join the world and use my advanced skill to do good. You see, I found from that very young age that almost anything was possible with the right scientific application. When I was in high school I was conducting experiments that most adults would be hard pressed to match. Then, being fully educated, I found I had a scientific knowledge and ability that rivaled anyone on the planet. I was ready to apply the science at my command to help the lives of those around me. My mark in history would be how much I would be able to improve the world we live in."

"Well, I hate to tell you, but you've really missed the mark there," Titan said, under his breath. Evidently, it had been loud enough for Dr. Melodian to hear.

Another surge of electricity coursed through the cords. Dr. Melodian's face was drawn tightly, his eyes narrowed to slits as he watched Titan convulse.

"Now, where was…ah yes," Dr. Melodian said, a faint smile returning to his face. "I worked at a couple of firms advancing their technology and helping them make huge profits, but it wasn't what I truly wanted to be doing. Then, General Stevenson paid me a visit. He made big promises and offered me all that I had ever wanted.

"I suddenly found myself in a lab with limitless resources and funding. I was paid more than I could spend, and I was working on projects and inventions that would help people. Or so I thought at least.

"You see they only told me what they thought I wanted to hear. They were taking all of the technologies that I was creating and perverting them for their own ill-conceived notions that mostly consisted of creating some form of weapon with the intention of killing people. This went on without my knowledge for decades. I was given false intelligence and false reports on my new creations upon their implementation.

"I created a system for delivering food and aid to third world nations when in fact they were using it to distribute arms to other groups with similar political interests. I built a system to deliver irrigation to crops, only to discover that it was mutated into a way to disperse toxic gases. You see, they would give me one set of instructions. I would in turn create a new piece of technology. Then, they had a whole other team ready and waiting to take my creations and turn them into some sort of weapon or machine to either end life or make it miserable to some other group of people. They were taking my life's work and perverting it, destroying my own true legacy."

Dr. Melodian paused, waiting for a response from Titan. When none came the cables suddenly began to bind even tighter causing Titan to gasp sharply for air.

"I don't know what to tell you," Titan said at last, gasping for air while his head hung nearly in his lap. "It's awful what they did to you, how they manipulated you, but it's still no reason to take it out on this city. If anything, you should have gone after their military bases or something."

"You speak blindly only because you have not heard the rest. You see, once I found out what they were doing I approached the general about it. I asked why it was being done, and I was simply told that it was in the best interest of the nation and the rest of the free world. I told him that no matter the reason, I could not be part of causing harm to others. From then on I found myself on the outside looking in. Communication to me became very one way. My own concerns, comments or suggestions were no longer heard. Instructions simply came to me by message or email," Dr. Melodian complained.

"It was not long after, when I first showed my reluctance for what they were doing with my creations, that I was suddenly brought up for review. They were deeming me incompetent. They used the fact that others were altering my work, saying that they had to hire others to complete the jobs that I could not. I was relieved of my duties. All of the rights and ownership of my work remained with the military. I also found myself unable to find further employment due to the fraudulent personnel record they created. They took everything from me, and now I am taking back!" Dr. Melodian declared.

"This still doesn't make any sense. You're going against everything that you used to stand for by attacking the city like this," Titan said, bracing his body for another shock.

Titan you are wasting your time trying to reason with this man. You must find a way out of this.

"You see what they have driven me to?" Dr. Melodian declared loudly. "They took everything from me. They had me doing work that was causing harm to others. Now I will force them to watch as I cause harm to one of their own cities, and then I will take it from them altogether!"

Suddenly, the console Dr. Melodian sat at began to rise into the air in front of Titan. It hovered in front of him five feet off the ground. The console transformed into a hover craft, powered by some form of jet propulsion from beneath. The cables binding Titan extended so that he remained in the same position. Openings suddenly appeared on various parts of the exterior of the console. A variety of weapons popped out of the openings; massive machine guns, arms with missiles, and a variety of other weapons.

"They will now feel the full extent of my wrath!" Dr. Melodian bellowed.

A hole suddenly opened in the roof directly above Dr. Melodian. The hovering console then flew upwards through the roof. Titan could see where the hover jets under the console. The cords continued to extend with Titan tightly bound until there was a loud click and the cords drew taught.

"Uh, oh…" was all Titan was able to utter before he found himself yanked up through the hole in the ceiling trailing the console as it flew through the dark passage.

Titan, you must get released.

Azure's plea went unanswered. Titan was trying his best to free at least one hand as he soared upward. He was bounced off the sides of the passage while being dragged along. He finally managed to wriggle one hand free. He was just able to reach out far enough to touch the wall as he bounced back and forth. He let it scrape along the side of the passage. It was a smooth metal surface with nothing to grab hold.

Then there was a loud crash as sunlight broke through the ceiling above. Chunks of metal and concrete rained down around Titan. He could see Dr. Melodian in his flying console soar into the blue sky above. Then, Titan broke through to the surface himself. He had only the briefest of moments to looks around to get his bearings before he was dragged further into the air behind Dr. Melodian.

He thought it still looked like he was in downtown Delta City, but was not quite sure. Skyscrapers and high-rises towered all around him. Titan dangled wildly, thirty feet behind the console. They soared over streets and buildings until Titan saw the military set up below where he had started. Suddenly, explosions of various sizes erupted in the street below. Just as he was registering that Dr. Melodian was firing at General Stevenson and his men, the console darted left and Titan kept veering right at the end of his cable. He crashed through the side of a glass front business tower.

Titan landed hard on the floor amidst a carpet of glass and rolled to a brief stop. He continued to work frantically at getting his arms free. Then, he was once again yanked forward. He was dragged on his back through the building, crashing through office walls and desks as he went. Suddenly, he was pulled up so hard he flipped right over onto his stomach and was then ripped through another window and into nothing but the open air.

Titan breached the sky once again, and he saw that Dr. Melodian's console was bobbing and weaving over the city firing missiles and machine gun blasts randomly. He was still helplessly bound with only one hand poking through the cables at his wrist. As he looked up he saw Dr. Melodian glance back at him for a moment, an evil grin on his face. Then, suddenly, he was once again being hurled toward a building. This one was tall and brick. Titan did his best to brace himself and prepare for the crash.

He crashed into the brick wall sending out an explosion of concrete. Titan opened his eyes and was rolling around on the floor of the building when he saw that it was another empty office space. He also noticed that some slack had been given to the cable from the crash. He managed to get his right arm free of the bindings. The cables once again tightened and he started to get dragged back toward the opening in the wall.

Using his free arm, Titan was able to loosen the bindings enough that he could move his legs and other arm around. He was nearly free from the cables altogether. Titan saw Dr. Melodian hovering in the distance through the hole in the wall. He darted downward rocketing the console toward the street. When the cables began to pull Titan back out through the opening, he was able to stand and plant his feet against the brick and grab the cables with his freed hands. He pulled up on them as hard as he could and suddenly Dr. Melodian reappeared. As the console corrected itself Titan shook loose the remaining bindings and grabbed his staff.

"AH... if it took you that long to escape those then how do you think you can stop me?" Dr. Melodian bellowed from the hovering console. Titan couldn't be sure, but it seemed that Dr. Melodian was enjoying himself and amused that Titan was free.

"Well, I guess you'll find out in a minute, won't you?" Titan answered, trying to sound angry and defiant, despite his tired and weakened state. Although, he could already feel his power replenishing, he did not feel fully healed and re-powered.

Dr. Melodian hit a couple of buttons on his control panel and the massive machine guns mounted on the console suddenly shifted and pointed at Titan. Titan quickly ducked low and started to run just as bullets started to shred through the building. The bullets ripped through desks, office cubicles, and walls. Plaster, wood, chunks of brick, and papers were sent flying everywhere. Missiles then hit the side of the building, shaking it to its foundations and blowing more big holes out of the building.

Titan could see Dr. Melodian hovering and bobbing around the side of the building trying to locate Titan. He glanced back to where he had been standing and spotted the console's cables still lying on the floor. Titan could see that Dr. Melodian had no idea where he was, and then saw his opening.

He ran to the cables and grabbed hold of the bindings with both hands and yanked down on them as hard as he could, and then he pulled them hard to the right. The hovering console suddenly darted downward, spinning wildly as it did.

He felt the cables draw tight as Dr. Melodian attempted to retract them. Titan pulled and ripped at the cords until they fell loose from his body at last. He grabbed his staff in one hand and walked to the edge of the opening in the wall. Dr. Melodian had dropped down at least thirty feet below him. The console veered around the corner of the building as Dr. Melodian tried to regain control. Using all of his power, Titan held onto the cables, afraid of what would happen if he let go. Then the console shot back out into view and began to rise up to his level.

Suddenly, an old all too familiar sound filled the air. Titan glanced up and saw that the military helicopter was now two stories above him and taking aim at Dr. Melodian. Titan saw the missiles and machine guns from the console suddenly aim toward the helicopter and knew there was just as much likelihood of the helicopter being struck first as there was Dr. Melodian. Titan moved immediately to intervene.

He launched himself out of the opening in the building and tried to angle his body right at the console as it sped up toward him. Dr. Melodian was so intent on the helicopter, he never saw Titan coming. He fired two missiles at the helicopter just as Titan collided with the console. The collision was just enough to send the missiles off course as they veered to the right and up into the clear blue sky exploding in a fiery ball.

Titan was latched onto to the back of the console which bucked and pitched as he struggled to hold on and gain a foothold. Dr. Melodian was attempting to turn and face him but couldn't turn all the way. The arms that held the machine guns also tried to turn and fire at Titan, but they were unable to take aim so close. Titan barely had a grip with his fingers digging in as much as they could, but his legs dangled dangerously below. He could not get a grip for his foot.

"You think you can stop me even from here? I will show you, you are nothing more than a gnat to me!" Dr. Melodian bellowed at Titan. Titan could only continue to cling desperately to the console.

Titan, you must disable this device before he is able to knock you off. If you cannot, and he gets away, you may not have another chance.

Just as Azure spoke, a big metal claw popped out of an opening right next to his face. Titan lost the hold of his left hand. He tried to dodge the claw and found himself dangling precariously by only one hand. The claw swung around and clubbed him on the side of the head. He lost grip with his other hand and began to slide down the side of the console. He finally gripped the bottom edge with his fingertips. From there he saw the array of lights and circuits up close for the first time that made the console fly. Titan gripped with his right hand tightly. He quickly made a fist with his left hand, then rammed it up through the base of the console with all his might.

The console pitched hard, down and to the right as he pulled out a handful of cables and circuitry. The console began to nosedive from three stories up and headed toward the street below. Dr. Melodian could be heard screaming with rage as the console plummeted. Titan hung on as long as he could before dropping off the console all together. He felt the rush of air caress him while falling toward the street below. His body twist and he was then looking up into the sky, waiting. Then, everything went black.

CHAPTER 14: Death From Below

Titan blacked out momentarily as he crashed onto the roof of a sports car from three stories up. He felt the sharp poking metal jab at him and the contour of the seats bending his back into unnatural positions. As he groggily opened his eyes, several armed policemen stood over him with guns drawn, aimed right at his head.

"Don't move, you're under arrest!" one of the officers said, when he saw Titan's eyes open.

Titan froze, the only muscle he let move were his eyes which darted all around looking for a route of escape. He saw none. He also became suddenly aware that he couldn't tell where his staff was and that he could not see or hear any signs of Dr. Melodian, so he had no way of knowing if he had been caught or not. Suddenly Chief Ross came into view. Chief Ross put his hand on the gun of the officer who was reading Titan his rights, forcing him to lower it. In his other hand he held a pair of handcuffs.

"I think we should help the man up so we can arrest him. What do you think Kowalski?" Chief Ross said, handing the hand-cuffs to the officer.

Ross then held his hand out to Titan in a gesture to help him out of the dilapidated car. With his joints and back aching he crawled off the car wreckage while grasping the Chief's hand. Once off, Titan slowly stretched out fully on his feet. He stood there momentarily face to face with Chief Ross.

"You're not as big up close as I thought you would be, you know," Chief Ross said to Titan.

"Yeah, I get that a lot," Titan answered.

Titan's eyes darted briefly all around his surroundings looking for an opening of escape. He noticed his staff lying in the middle of the street. He also saw the wreckage of a building that a group of military men were now descending upon. He could only assume that was where Dr. Melodian had crashed with his console.

"I'm sorry, but we have to take you in," Chief Ross said to Titan.

"I'm sorry too, because I can't let you do that," Titan replied, once again locking eyes with Chief Ross. Titan's glare never broke while taking several slow steps and bent to scoop up his staff.

Chief Ross's eyes narrowed at Titan's decree. Titan noticed the other officers flanking him slowly begin to raise their weapons once again. Chief Ross clearly saw this gesture from his men, but did not stop them this time.

"Look, we appreciate all you've done here, but the law is still the law," Chief Ross said.

"That's right, I want this man arrested immediately!" came a voice from behind

Chief Ross whirled around quickly and saw Mayor Winfield charging forward. His clothes were disheveled and his hair standing out all over. His young assistant was at his heels like a loyal dog.

"Mayor Winfield, what are you doing here? How did you get through?" Chief Ross demanded to know.

"I'm the mayor. I need to be where the people of this city need me."

"Well, this is a police matter and you are not needed here now," said Chief Ross.

"Arrest this man. He is a menace, and has been terrorizing this city for nearly a year now," Mayor Winfield said, clearly ignoring Chief Ross.

Chief Ross again locked eyes with Titan. He raised the handcuffs in his hand and took a step forward with a regretful look on his face. Titan raised his hands shoulder level cautiously and began to look for an escape route as fast as he could that would ensure everyone's safety. Before he could take another step, however, General Stevenson suddenly stepped into view and stopped right in front of Chief Ross. Chief Ross stopped and took a sudden step back so as not to collide with the general.

"Chief, I would like to recommend that you don't go through with that," General Stevenson said, pointing to the cuff in Ross's hands.

"What? You can't do that," Mayor Winfield said, stepping forward his face flushing red with anger. "You promised me that you would take care of the Titan situation."

"No, Mayor, I told you that if he got in our way dealing with Melodian that we would eliminate him as a threat. He hasn't been in our way, however. In fact, he's helped us a great deal. My men are now trying to locate the neutralized threat in that ruined building, and we can do that because of the help we've had from Titan."

General Stevenson then turned back to Chief Ross.

"So, Chief, you've got a choice here. You can arrest the hero of the city or you can let him go now," General Stevenson said.

Chief Ross looked over at Titan then at the mayor, then down at the cuffs in his hand.

"I know it's no easy decision, especially with all the emotions at play with these events, but I do believe the city is still under lockdown, is that right, Chief?" General Stevenson asked.

Chief Ross lowered his head in deep thought. He then slid the cuffs back into his pocket and raised his head.

"You're right, General. Under these extraordinary circumstances I say that these acts of Titan's were done under order of the Delta City Police to aid in ending this threat to our great city." Chief Ross then turned his gaze from Titan to the mayor. "Titan is free to go." He then quickly shot it back to Titan. "For now, do you understand? This is no permanent free pass."

Titan nodded his head slowly in wide-eyed disbelief.

"No! I demand that this man be ar...," Mayor Winfield began.

The mayor was cut off suddenly by a commotion behind them. Workers at the building wreckage where Dr. Melodian had crashed his console were sent scattering. The rubble was shaking and trembling causing large pieces of debris to roll down into the street below. Then, Dr. Melodian crashed through the debris with his console sealed tight in a glass dome that covered the top, protecting him. The console had black smoke pouring from the back of it. Sparks flickered and flashed where Titan had rammed his fist through. The console bobbed and weaved trying to stay in the air, until it finally paused, hovering fifteen feet above the street where Titan and the others stood. The dome retracted and Dr. Melodian faced them all.

"Did you think that I would be stopped so easily? My wrath has only just begun!" Dr. Melodian bellowed.

Suddenly the ground began to tremble. Titan readied his staff and prepared to fire a lightning blast at Dr. Melodian. Everyone else braced themselves, unsure of what was about to happen. Suddenly the sewer grate in the middle of the street popped off, and hordes of Spiderbots emerged from the depths of the underground. They were all the same types that Titan had faced in the sewer not long ago. The horde became so big the sewer hole could not contain it and the street began to crumble away leaving a massive hole behind. The Spiderbots were moving in such mass numbers that they were able to move together over vehicles and up walls like a tsunami. All of them would work together like one big wave toward their goal, which seemed to be to consume the city. The Spiderbots immediately began firing in every direction.

Titan fired a blast of lightning at the console just as Dr. Melodian darted out of his sights. Titan ran forward trying to sidestep the Spiderbots to get to Dr. Melodian. The console was rocketing straight down at the hole left by the Spiderbots. Titan dove toward the opening trying to intercept Melodian, but the horde rose around him, in one giant wave, rising around him.

Titan's world went dark beneath the horde. He still gripped his staff and began to fire blasts of lightning. He could hear the sizzle and crackle of the blasts tearing through the Spiderbot wave around him. At last Titan was standing in the middle of the street with destroyed Spiderbots littered all around him. Dr. Melodian was nowhere to be seen.

Titan glanced to the edge of the street where he had left Chief Ross and General Stevenson. They and their men had retreated into a small diner to avoid the swarm. Titan made his way toward the diner. He hunched over and drew his staff close to him, swinging it viciously at any of the Spiderbots that blocked his path. At last he reached the diner and entered, leaving the chaos behind.

Titan's uniform was in complete ruins. Despite his advanced healing, Titan had many visible bruises and cuts covering much of his body. He had dried blood smeared over his body from many of the cuts he received earlier that had already healed over.

"Did you get him?" General Stevenson asked. He stood behind the counter facing his men and Chief Ross. Both hands forming into fists planted firmly on the counter holding his weight. A dozen other soldiers were all around the diner.

Titan shook his head.

"We need to get out there. Stop these things," Chief Ross said. Panic could be heard in his voice for the first time.

"We don't even know how these things work. There could be a central processing unit producing them that we could take out. Or we could just be swimming upstream, and without Melodian in our hands, we don't know if we can even stop them," General Stevenson replied.

"I faced some of these things in the sewer. It seemed like they were just some advanced artificial intelligence that ran on their own. I think we can just wipe them out. I also know where Melodian's base is underground. I'm sure we could track him from there," Titan chimed in. He had sheathed his staff and was half walking half limping toward General Stevenson.

"Well, that sounds like a good start to me. Let's pulverize these things, and then take the offensive against the good doctor, any objections?" General Stevenson asked, turning toward Chief Ross and Mayor Winfield.

Chief Ross stood in the middle of the diner staring out the window as the Spiderbots scurried through the streets firing their weapons at unseen targets. Mayor Winfield sat at a booth against the far wall. His head hung down over the table and continued to shake in disbelief, his assistant, Jeffery, stood by his side. The mayor said nothing, he wouldn't even look over at the general or Titan, as though not seeing them there made none of this real. Chief Ross, however, finally broke away from the window and turned toward them.

"Let's do it!" Chief Ross said. "I can have my men lay down a perimeter to try and contain these things. Can you get yours deployed over the area and take some out?"

"I most certainly can," General Stevenson replied.

"Good. Can we count on you to help with this?" Chief Ross asked, turning right toward Titan now.

Titan said nothing at first. He wasn't even sure that it was him that Chief Ross was speaking to. Once he understood, he replied.

"Of course, all I've ever done is try and protect this city and I'm not going to stop doing that now, when it needs me the most," Titan answered.

"Okay then, gentlemen, let's get down to business," General Stevenson said, pulling up a M16 rifle from below the counter, holding it up high. "Let's get ready to move out men!"

General Stevenson grabbed a walkie-talkie from a nearby soldier and began giving commands through it. Chief Ross pulled out his cell and started to do the same. Mayor Winfield never moved from his bench. He had gone from a look of disbelief to one of complete fear. His skin had gone a pale hue and beads of sweat could be seen along his hairline.

"Mr. Mayor, I suggest you and your assistant wait here for things to blow over," Chief Ross said, walking toward the door. Jeffery nodded at Ross, but Mayor Winfield never looked up.

The soldiers lined up on either side of the door with weapons drawn and ready. Chief Ross and General Stevenson stood next to the men. Titan stood back a couple feet and was facing the door head on. The soldiers were all poised to attack the Spiderbot chaos outside, but Stevenson and Ross were both looking back at Titan.

"I'm the one with superpowers so I'll go out first," Titan said, pulling out his staff once again.

No one replied. General Stevenson simply turned and grabbed hold of the door. He looked back at Titan and nodded. Titan nodded back and then Stevenson pulled the door open wide.

Titan burst through the open door while firing off a blast of lightning to clear the way. There were hundreds of Spiderbots crawling over the area. It was like one big rolling wave of dark metal. Titan swung his staff at three bots that turned and came at him. His staff connected and they flew through the air in smashed pieces. He continued to move forward doing much of the same. He would fire and then take a swipe or two while moving forward deeper into the horde. Up close he could see the individual Spiderbots, but as a group they appeared as one wave working together to destroy. Titan sent more of them sailing into crushed oblivion, when the wave seemed to direct itself toward him trying to engulf him and eliminate the threat against them.

A wave of Spiderbots suddenly rose up over his head to his right, Titan looked back to see how the others were doing. They had all formed a tight phalanx, and were firing at the bots at a rapid pace. Together they seemed to be able to hold off the onslaught of Spiderbots that threatened to take over. Bullets soaring through the air never had to go far before finding a target. They sliced through the bots easily and they were instantly destroyed.

The wave of Spiderbots crashed down on Titan and began to sweep him away. It was like being pulled away by the tide. He gripped his staff with all his might as it threatened to come loose and wash away. He pulled it in tight and let the wave of Spiderbots pull him where it may. Gathering all of his power, he coursed it through his staff and fired off the biggest blast of lightning that he could muster. Spiderbots were sent flying everywhere. The blast either seemed to disable the bots or blow them to pieces. Either was fine with Titan, as long as the horde was dispersed.

Titan quickly jumped to his feet, still clutching his staff tightly, as the horde broke away. Several bots lunged at him and he batted them away with his staff. He turned back to the phalanx of soldiers and saw that they were still tightly grouped as they ploughed their way through much of the horde. Now only a few dozen bots remained. The military helicopters had also pulled in low and were firing at the Spiderbot horde in the streets. The fact that they seemed to be massing together made them easier targets all around. Spiderbot carcasses littered the entire area.

"We did it!" Titan exclaimed, gazing around at all of the crushed and shattered Spiderbots.

Fires had erupted in several areas and the fronts of some buildings lay in ruin. Most of the damage, however, seemed to be contained within this one street. Several soldiers and police officers went around firing single rounds into the few Spiderbots that were still somewhat operational. General Stevenson and Chief Ross had convened in the middle of the street just fifteen yards from where Titan now stood. Both men were simultaneously talking to each other while pointing at various trouble spots where damage was done and then speaking into their own respective phones as they gave orders to their men.

Do not celebrate prematurely. The true villain is still at large, and may already be planning on coming to you.

"Don't worry; I know we still have to get Melodian, but seriously, what else could be left?"

Suddenly, the ground began to tremble and shake. Loosened cinder blocks and brick fell from already damaged buildings and crashed into the street or sidewalk where they broke into pieces. The tremors were so powerful that everyone, including Titan, struggled to stay on their feet. Titan glanced down between his feet and saw a crack appear in the asphalt. It spread and widened right before his eyes. The ground then began to pull apart and shift. Everyone started to run toward the doorways.

Titan took several steps away from the crack in the street and watched cautiously as it continued to widen. The crack then joined several others that had formed in the street and suddenly the ground began to give away and massive chunks of asphalt fell inward. Then, a metal object began to emerge from the hole. It continued to rise into the air amidst a cloud of debris that obscured Titan's view of the object. As the dust cleared and the ground ceased to shake, Titan found himself staring at a massive robot. He took his gaze from its base up its one hundred foot body to its summit. He quickly realized it was a giant robot he was looking at. In what was its head, Titan could see Dr. Melodian at the controls. Melodian looked down over the city from the robot's eyes, a delightfully mad grin smeared across his face.

"I am Dr. Karl Melodian," He bellowed through a loudspeaker. The sound echoed down the corridor of the city streets. "And now you will feel my wrath!"

CHAPTER 15: One Hundred Feet of Terror

Titan could only stare at the massive robot in a mixture of terror and wonder. He braced himself, waiting to strike, but also afraid of what might happen if he were struck back. Dirt and bits of the underground continued to tumbles from the giant robot and fall to earth. The street grew relatively quiet. Everyone stood frozen, watching, waiting for it to move. Suddenly, the noise of whirring machine parts and grinding metal filled the air as the robot took a step forward and began to march down the street.

"Open fire!" General Stevenson roared, stepping back into the street right behind the robot and began to unload his gun along its back.

Soldiers and police officers along the street began to follow suit, although none ventured as closely to the robot as the general. The bullets seemed to not even dent its metal hide. Titan took aim and fired off two quick powerful blasts connecting with its hip and neck joints and left only a black scorch mark. Both military helicopters then swooped in with a barrage of gunfire before each launched missiles at it as they passed on either side and then soared back up overhead. Once the fire cloud dissipated the damage was minimal and the robot continued.

The helicopters swung around and began to make another approach. Gunfire from the ground troops continued to pound fruitlessly at the massive machine. As the helicopters came in again and prepared to fire, each of the robots long arms rose up and swatted the helicopters from the sky like flies. The helicopters crumbled like paper planes and crashed into the side of buildings spilling shattered glass and crushed brick to the street below.

Titan, this is what I have feared. Such a destructive machine could cause untold damage to this city.

"Yeah, tell me about it."

You must stop it at once. Only you have the power to end this madness.

"I figured you'd say something like that. I just don't want to end up like a bug on the bottom of its shoe," Titan said.

If you utilize all of your powers and abilities you will be fine, and this madness can end.

Ahead, the giant robot lumbered on, approaching the police barricade laid across the road. The police were firing at it at will. Bullets pinged and ricocheted off the metal machine. When it became clear that they had no hope of stopping or even slowing the giant, they were forced to abandon their position and head for cover. Then, one arm of the giant robot raised and aimed itself at the line of police cars. The hand separated from the bottom of the wrist, lifting up on a hinge, and three missiles came firing out. They connected with the police cruisers and sent them into fiery heaps of molten metal. The robot still did not hesitate as Dr. Melodian steered it right through the blaze that lined the street and continued into Delta City.

"Well, that's definitely my cue," Titan said racing forward in the wake of the massive robot.

Titan raced down the center of the street hurdling over abandoned cars and wreckages as he went. Once he felt in range he pulled out his staff and braced himself as he fired a lightning blast at the machine. He mustered all the power that he could summon to the staff as it fired. The blast struck the robot square in the back. It stopped suddenly; a smoking black scorch mark was left on its metal back.

The robot slowly began to turn to face Titan. Titan, despite the nerves that were threatening to make his knees buckle over completely, stood his ground, braced and ready, yet unsure where to strike next. He looked up and could see the mad, delighted grin of Dr. Melodian in the cockpit looking out of the robot's head. He was frantically grabbing at levers and pushing at buttons with a child's zeal. Then, both long arms reached out and both hands popped up this time as a barrage of missiles fired out at Titan.

Nearly a dozen white smoke trails sailed over the street making their way to Titan.

He turned and blindly leaped away as fast as he could. He was barely five feet in the air, however, when the missiles crashed into the street in a massive fire ball. Heat engulfed Titan as the force of the blast launched him ahead like a rocket. He had no control over his direction and began to flail about wildly trying to slow himself. Then, he crashed through a storefront window, plowing through racks of clothing and apparel. He finally crash landed into the counter, leaving it a pile of scrap wood.

Titan tried to get to his feet as he crawled out of the debris of the front counter. Bits of glass and wood fell from him. A tattered pair of pants clung to his shoulder, and as he peeled them off he glanced into one of the viewing mirrors and saw himself for the first time. He was shirtless now. What was left of his shirt hung down from his waist over his belt. His pants were littered with holes. His gloves were mostly in tact but still sported several holes as well. His mask had some major holes and tears, where his hair now hung out. He wondered if it even hid his identity at all anymore. Over his arms, chest and stomach was smears and lines of blood. He was not even aware what blood was fresh and which was from cuts that had already healed over.

He glanced in to the bottom corner of the mirror and saw a frightened middle aged man crouching down and gazing at him from the back of the store. Titan turned and began to walk toward the man. He could hear the robot once again making its way through the city outside.

"What are you still doing here?" Titan asked as he approached the man.

"I couldn't just leave my store, it means everything to me," the man replied. He was bald on top with a ring of rich black hair. He had a long thin nose and a pencil thin moustache. He was dressed in a purple collared shirt, tie and a black vest. He still had a long measuring tape draped around his neck. His eyes were wide and his jaw continued to move, but no more words would come out.

"Look, it's not safe," Titan said. The man simply nodded, bewildered, and began to walk out the front door.

"No, that's not what I meant. I meant you shouldn't have stayed, but now that you have you may as well stay in here. Just try and stay out of sight. I think that thing has moved on anyway," suggested Titan.

The man simply nodded again. He stood there staring at Titan. It was then that Titan realized the impact of the battle at hand. He knew then that he had to stop Dr. Melodian at all costs. Titan was about to leave when he noticed the man was not moving. He shot the man a stern look and pointed toward the back of the store. The man nodded furiously, his slack jaw dangling away. After a brief moment he finally turned and shuffled to the back of his tailor shop.

Titan ran through the debris of the now destroyed shop and stepped back into the street. He saw the robot in the distance. Its arms were out and columns of smoke rose into the air. He could hear people scream as it moved on, away from the protected area the military and police had tried to create. Titan ran forward before leaping into the air. He stayed to the street for now, taking big, block-length leaps into the air. He looked below as he followed the swath of destruction left by Dr. Melodian.

Cars were either crushed or ablaze. Buildings had randomly had their fronts swiped off. Several appeared to have had missiles fired into them. Six blocks up, he saw a line of two tanks that had been shredded, their husks spouting plumes of flame. He saw no sign of any people, which he took as a good sign.

"Azure, I have no idea what I can do to take this thing down. It's just too big and too powerful," Titan said, drawing closer to the robot, and nearly within range.

Do not be fooled by the illusion of its size. It is still only a machine. It has strength in its size, but you have a far larger arsenal at your disposal.

As usual, Titan was only vaguely aware of what any of that could mean. He did not answer, however. The scene he saw ahead as he drew close suddenly changed everything.

Just over a block away, Titan saw the robot stopped in front of a group of onlookers who had been unable to get away from its wrath. It had one foot raised in the air and was about to bring it down on two people cowering on the sidewalk. One of the people was Vicki Earnhardt. She had her arms wrapped around an elderly woman, and Titan realized that she had been helping the woman to safety when the robot turned on them.

Titan moved at alarming speed toward the dropping metal foot. In a blink, he found himself staring down at Vicki, whose eyes were closed tight waiting for the inevitable. She opened her eyes, looking at Titan in disbelief. He was down on one knee with his arms raised in the air, his hands clutching the edges of the robot's foot. The sound of the robot's gears grinding away echoed through the street as it tried to crush Titan, and everyone, under it. Titan's arms trembled under the pressure. He breathed in sharp quick breaths with his teeth gritted tightly.

"What, you couldn't just wait for me to bring this one to you?" Titan asked her.

Vicki fell backwards her arms reaching back to stop herself. Her eyes wide, she was panting furiously while staring at Titan. It was the first time she had ever needed to be saved by him since they had met at her apartment all those months ago.

"Move, Now! Hurry!" Titan said, in a strained voice as loud as he could to Vicki.

For a moment Vicki just sat there propped up on her arms staring. Then she nodded, collected herself and the elderly woman and quickly scuttled her to safety to the closest building. Two men were waving them in while holding the door open. They quickly shut it once they were both secured inside.

The robot's foot continued to press down, inching ever closer to the pavement. Titan felt his body compressing and giving away under the pressure. The foot now mostly rested along his back while his arms just could not seem to hold up on their own. His staff lay on the ground at his feet and completely out of reach. He knew he had to act fast or be crushed.

Acting out of desperation, Titan quickly brought one tightly coiled fist down before throwing it back up at the bottom of the robot's foot with all his might. The foot dented inward and jerked back from the blow. Titan then began to push up with all his strength and then brought his fist down, ready to strike again. This time the same dent was made bigger, and Titan noticed a small crack form in the metal. He quickly punched it again three more times. Then, on the last punch, his fist rammed right through the metal. When he pulled it out he had a fistful of wires and circuits clutched in his hand. Suddenly the leg of the robot lifted enough to free Titan from it.

As the foot jerked and writhed, Titan bent and scooped up his staff. With the robot's one leg raised, he leaped at the other leg with his staff out. Just at the point of impact, Titan fired a blast into the robot's knee joint. As soon as he landed back on the ground, he pushed against it with all his might. The robot toppled backward, its arm swiping sideways taking out a whole row of windows and bricks off of buildings. It landed on its back with a thunderous crash making the ground tremble like it had been shaken by a massive earthquake.

Titan stood for a moment in disbelief. Instantly, the robot's flailing limbs were moving and trying to lift itself back to its feet. Titan quickly picked up his staff and leaped into the air. He curled his body into a tight ball, and then brought his staff down with all the force he could muster as he landed onto the chest of the robot. The bottom of the staff pierced the robot's armor like a knife. Then, he flipped the staff around and fired a lightning blast directly at its insides. An array of sparks and electrical current erupted from the chest cavity. Amidst the eruption, Titan reached in and began to yank out any circuitry he could get his hands on. Thick black smoke began to pour from every crack or opening on the robot.

Titan stood and looked toward the head of the machine. Something there was trying to move. Titan began to walk cautiously along the robot toward the head where Dr. Melodian was. While approaching, he saw that Melodian was no longer at the cockpit. Just as he reached the area the top of the head, a hatch flew open like the lid of a cookie jar and Dr. Melodian's console came sputtering out attempting an escape.

The console came out several feet off the ground still showing much of the damage it received earlier. It smoked and sputtered, but before it could get any farther Titan grabbed the back edge with his right hand. He vaulted over the top of it and brought his other hand down directly at Melodian's control panel. It buzzed and crackled as Titan rendered it inoperative. The console crashed to the street. Titan continued to pummel it. Dr. Melodian wrapped his arms around his head to protect against the onslaught until Titan stood, panting and heaving, his fists swaying at his sides.

Suddenly, three green jeeps came to a screeching halt right around the husk of the giant robot. General Stevenson and Chief Ross got out of the one that was closest, and came over to Titan.

"Keep him away from me! Stop him!" Dr. Melodian pleaded when he saw Stevenson approach.

"You've lost all right to ask for anything, even protection," General Stevenson said, as he came right up to Melodian.

He put one hand out toward Ross not taking his eyes off Melodian. Ross slipped a pair of handcuffs onto his hands without even having to be asked. The general then cuffed Melodian and signaled to another group of soldiers to come in.

"Men, get the good doctor out of here, will you?" Stevenson ordered.

"Yes sir," the three soldiers said in unison and moved in.

Stevenson then turned to Titan.

"Sorry, we kind of left you holding the bag there, kid," General Stevenson said. "Things got a little out of hand pretty quickly and we had to regroup. Then we had to catch up."

"It's just as well. There was no sense in any of your men getting hurt. I saw the wreckage back there. Were your men all right?" Titan asked.

"Some are a little banged up, but they'll all live," Stevenson answered. He then looked over at Ross.

"All our men are accounted for. I think we have you to thank for some of that too," Chief Ross said.

"So, what now?" Titan asked.

There was silence, as the three of them seemed to assess the situation and each other.

"Well, we'll be leaving town, with Dr. Melodian in our custody. He will stand trial for all of his crimes, which are many. I don't think you will be hearing from him for some time," General Stevenson said.

Titan then looked over at Ross.

"It's really too hard to tell what the future holds now," Chief Ross said. "It will take some time for the city to recover from this and rebuild, but we will."

"That's not really what I meant," Titan responded.

"I know. Everything else is still too complicated. I know the mayor's office won't stop trying to pursue apprehending you. All I can say for the DCPD right now, is that your actions here today won't be forgotten any time soon. I think you've earned the rest of the day off. You should leave. We'll take it from here," Chief Ross said.

Titan nodded in thanks. He looked around as more police and military began to flood the area. Onlookers and reporters also started to appear from the periphery. Titan saw Vicki come out from the building she had been taking shelter. She mouthed the words thank you as they locked eyes. Titan only smiled and nodded back. He was about to take a step in her direction when people started to call out his name and come toward him. He took that as his cue. He leaped up to a nearby building and began to make his way back home.

That went very well.

"Yeah, except for all the damage and people that may have been hurt," Titan responded, soaring over the city toward the east end.

Yes, except for that, but you have taken a horrible situation, set it right and then used it to mend your relationship with the authorities of this city.

"Thanks," was all he said, but despite his battered body aching and feeling exhausted, he couldn't have agreed more with Azure

CHAPTER 16: Picking Up the Pieces

"Are you friend or family?" the woman at the hospital reception desk asked Michael.

"Um…family. He's my grandfather," Michael replied.

"Okay, one moment," she continued without even looking up. She was busy, furiously typing away at her keyboard. "It's room 308. Just turn down the hallway behind you to your left and use the bank of elevators there."

"Thank you," Michael said, as he began to turn away. Then, he suddenly turned back. "Can you tell me if there have been any other visitors to see him today?"

"Um…yes it seems there was one other visitor who was with him when he was checked in. Also a grandson it looks like," She said, looking back down at her computer.

"Thank you," Michael replied turning toward the elevators.

The hospital was quite a bit busier than when Michael had been there the other day. Many people were brought in with injuries resulting from the attacks by Dr. Melodian. In fact the city in general seemed quite a bit busier and more hectic than it did the day before. When Michael had transformed and gone back to the clinic to check in on his grandpa, it had taken him some time to find out that he had to been taken back to the hospital for observation.

As he made his way over, it seemed that the city-wide lockdown had already fallen to the wayside. However, with so many emergency vehicles making their way through the streets the city seemed to have gone from lockdown to gridlock. It had taken him nearly an hour to get from the clinic to the hospital.

On his way he had tried to call Carly but couldn't get through. He had sent her a text to at least let her know that he was alright. He could only imagine the questions that would get once he was face to face with her and Perminder.

Michael had had to weave his way through a tangle of people and medical staff to get to room 308, but at last he found it. Just as he was about to open the door and walk in, the door swung open and someone came out bumping into Michael. Something metal clanged to the ground and Michael bent to pick it up.

"Here you go, Vince," Michael said scooping up the keys and holding them out to Vince.

"You know that was a real loser move ditching Grandpa like that," Vince snarled back ignoring the keys in Michael's hands.

"I know, and thanks for coming down to bail me out. I really appreciate it," Michael replied, trying his best to stay level headed.

"He's been in there worried sick about you. And you think I disrespect him," Vince continued.

"I have no excuses, Vince. Thanks for coming down for him though, really," said Michael.

"Thanks," Vince said, finally snatching the keys from Michael's hand.

"No problem, what are brothers for?" Michael managed, with as little sarcasm as he could muster.

Vince started to walk away, but kept glancing back at Michael with narrow questioning gaze that seemed to eye him with suspicion. Michael only smiled back at him. Once Vince rounded the corner Michael walked into the room. There were only two beds in the room. Grandpa Dale was closest to the door. The curtain was drawn across, separating them from the other patient in the room.

"Hi Grandpa, how are you doing?" Michael asked, approaching the bed.

"Michael, I thought I heard your voice out there," Grandpa Dale said, reaching one hand out for Michael. "I'm glad you decided to take it easy on your brother. Although, if you wanted to start a fight with him, you're in the right place to do it."

Michael blushed as Grandpa Dale broke into a wide smile. He was glad to see it.

"Well, someone recently reminded me that I only have one brother, and that maybe I should try and be easier on him." Michael stepped up to the bed and grasped Grandpa Dale's outstretched hand and brought it in close.

"Must have been a pretty wise guy, huh?" said Grandpa Dale.

"Grandpa, look, I'm so sorry I had to leave like that," Michael began.

"There's no need to apologize," Grandpa Dale interjected. He shifted his hand in Michael's and ran his finger very carefully over the power ring on the middle finger of his right hand. "I'm sure you had some other pretty big responsibilities. Besides, I was in good hands."

Nothing more was spoken of it. Michael sat and visited with his grandfather as though they were back at home having a nice relaxing evening. Eventually they turned to watch the TV that was mounted in the upper corner of the room. The volume was on, but low. All channels were covering the events of downtown and the attacks of Dr. Melodian. Images kept flashing before them of the battle Titan had with the giant robot. Very little seemed to have been captured of the Spiderbot attack, what was mostly the aftermath. Then, images of clean up and rescue began to be shown. Michael was relieved to see that several people seemed to have been rescued from the lair of Dr. Melodian. Michael could only assume that this was the loved ones hammerhead had referenced. From there, coverage began to show the arrest of Sonic and Hawk, who had been found more or less where Titan had left them both.

On the screen Chief Ross was giving a summary of events and post-mortem of clean-up and charges that were being laid. There were some other city officials flanking the podium around Ross including Mayor Winfield. Michael looked, but General Stevenson was nowhere to be seen.

"Dr. Melodian is currently in military custody. The full extent of charges against him will be issued in coming days. I guarantee that he will pay for the crimes he has committed against Delta City," Chief Ross said sternly into the cameras.

"What about Titan? Is he still wanted by the DCPD?" came a voice from the throngs of reporters. The cameras panned and showed Vicki sitting in the second row, with her notepad open in hand. Michael made mental note to arrange one monster exclusive for his favorite reporter once he had the chance.

There was a slight pause as Ross looked down at the podium and cleared his throat. Michael leaned forward, not wanting to miss anything that was about to be said. Finally Ross looked back up and spoke.

"It was largely because of Titan that the damage to the city was kept to what it was. He was an enormous part of our capture of Dr. Melodian and all his men. He is still a citizen that is taking the law into his own hands, but I would say that in light of the events of today the DCPD will look favorably upon his actions as long as they continue to help the people of Delta City and keep it safe."

A furor broke amongst the reporters, but Ross gave them a slight nod and wave before stepping down from the podium and vanishing from sight. The mayor quickly jumped to the podium flushed red with anger at the remarks of Chief Ross.

"The damage this city has sustained is quite extensive, and Titan was there, a part of most of it," Mayor Winfield said, glaring at everyone in front of him. "Where is he now? Is he out there with all the first responders? Is he doing anything to help put this city back together? No, he's gone, leaving all the dirty work to us."

With a click, the TV suddenly went black.

"Well, I think that's enough of that, don't you?" Grandpa Dale said, the

TV remote in his hand. His fingers were still fumbling over the buttons. Then, he reached out, searching, for the rolling bedside table that seems to come with every hospital bed. He found it and rested the remote on top. He leaned back and yawned deeply.

"Grandpa, you need some rest. I'll come by tomorrow and be here to bring you home," Michael said.

"I'm fine, just fine. I just needed to stretch out my jaw muscles, that's all," said Grandpa Dale quietly.

"Well, I'm going to head home so you have a chance to stretch out your eyelids," Michael replied.

Michael said his goodbyes and then turned and walked out of the room. He felt better than he had in ages, walking the corridors of the hospital. The hospital itself was still bustling with activity from injured attack victims. All Michael could think of, as he walked through the hall and saw injured people lying on gurneys, was that it all could have been so much worse had Dr. Melodian not been stopped.

As he exited the hospital and made his way to the bus stop, the sun was shining and the warm air was comforting. His muscles still ached, but they seemed to be getting better each passing minute. He glanced at the ring, and it seemed to shine brightly with the blue gem sparkling and dancing with a particular brilliancy. Michael shoved his hands in his pocket so the ring would not draw any unwanted attention.

The bus ride back to the east side suddenly seemed like the most restful experience that he had had in a long time. He sent several quick texts to Carly and to Perminder and then spent the rest of the time staring out the bus window with the city rolling by. He found himself back in the neighborhood before he knew it.

He hit the sidewalk and began to walk to Carly's building lost in a sea of his own thoughts. He had made it half a block when the door to the Burger Pit suddenly swung open and he was nearly knocked over backwards. He stopped just short of knocking over their basket of fries and soda.

"Whoa, easy there," Michael began. He stopped suddenly when he found himself staring at Dave.

"Sorry about that. Oh, Mike, it's you." Dave said. "What, are you gonna chastise me for being here too?"

The sting of the words could be seen on Michael's face. He tried to hide his emotions from his friend.

"Dave, look, I'm sorry if I've been a bit of a jerk lately. I just know the kind of guy that Vince is. I also know the kind of people that he hangs around with," said Michael.

"What like Dylan? Come on, I don't think either of them are that bad," Dave interjected.

"Look, you're my friend, one of my best friends. I just don't want to see you find yourself in trouble. If you wanna hang out around Vince that's your business, just promise me that you'll be careful and not get yourself into any kind of trouble," said Michael.

Dave paused a moment, taken back by Michael's honesty.

"Don't worry, I'll be careful. You think I want Titan to be coming after me?" Dave said with a laugh. Michael tried his best to mimic a laugh of his own.

"Look, I'm on my way to Carly's, you want to join me?" Michael offered.

"Hey, I'd love to, it's been too long, but I have plans. Maybe later?" Dave casually evaded

"For sure, I'll catch you later then."

Michael watched as Dave walked down the street and turned out of sight. Then he turned and continued his way to Carly's. Once he arrived, she buzzed him in from the intercom and he bounded up the stairs to the rooftop where they were to meet. He burst through doorway and found Perminder and Carly sitting at the old patio set in the middle of the roof waiting for his arrival.

"Man, I thought you'd never show up," Perminder exclaimed.

Michael was unable to respond, Carly had instantly run from the table and leaped into his arms. Her soft lips pushed hard against his own as she kissed him. It was at that exact moment that the topsy turvy world Michael had been living in finally seemed to balance back into place.

"Oh, Michael, that was the worst thing I could ever have imagined doing. It was so awful to watch, and I was helpless not to be able to help you at all. I hated it," Carly said, her eyes tearing up, as she stared into Michael's eyes.

"Hey, it was also pretty awesome to watch. You kicked that thing's big metal butt," Perminder said from the table.

Michael took Carly by the hand and led her back over to the table. He then spent the next hour telling them the entire story. He told all about Hammerhead and the underground passage, and Melodian and the battle that ensued. Both sat in silent wonder as he told his story.

"Wow!" was all Perminder could muster once Michael had finished.

Carly said nothing. She simply reached out and took Michael's hand and pulled it in tight. Michael sat back in his chair and looked up to the sky, telling the story seemed to take the last of his energy.

"What's wrong?" Carly asked him.

"I just can't get over it. Dr. Melodian started out his life with such noble intentions. How could all of that potential have gone so horribly wrong?" wondered Michael.

"The guy had no one there to ground him," Perminder said. "At least you've got us. Carly and I are like your team, you know, backing you up and supporting you. She told me how she helped you with Mr. Midnight and the motion inhibitors. Maybe we can be like that. I know there wasn't a whole lot we could do this time, but there will be other times and we'll be there to help you. You don't have to go it alone."

So many thoughts swirled through Michael's head once Perminder said those words. He didn't know where to even begin. Then he looked over at Carly and saw her beaming confidently at him. At that moment there was only one thing on his mind. He turned back to Perminder and spoke.

"You're right. There will be more times where the city is in danger and Titan is needed. I won't be able to do it on my own all the time either. It's good to know I'll have a great team backing me up," Michael said with a broad smile.

ABOUT THE AUTHOR

Hugh Beckstead developed a lifelong love of superhero comics growing up across Eastern and Western Canada, which lead him to create a superhero world of his own with Titan.

He currently lives in Kelowna British Columbia with his wife Carly and son Brayden. TITAN: City Under Siege is his second book in the TITAN series.